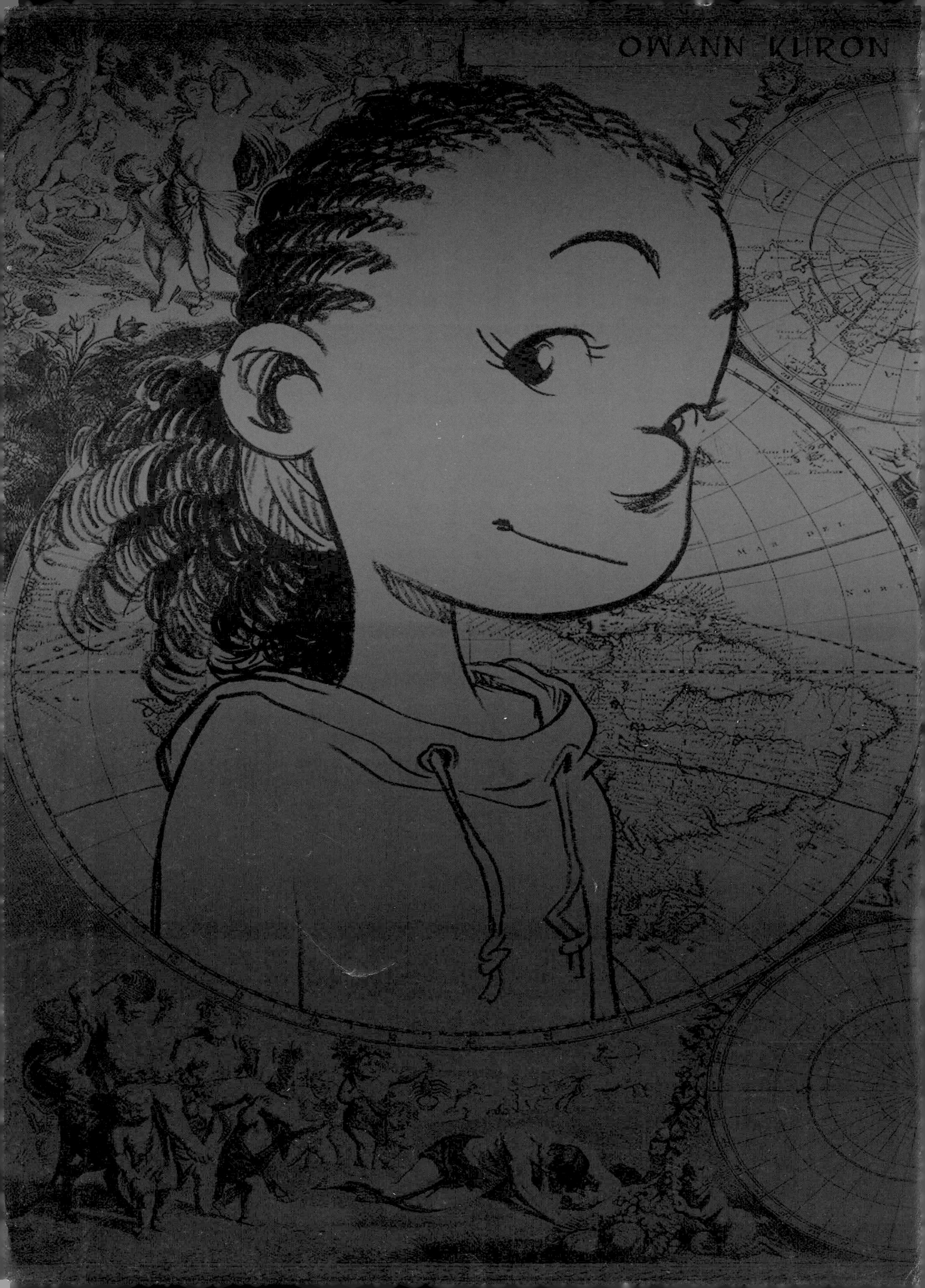
OWANN KURON

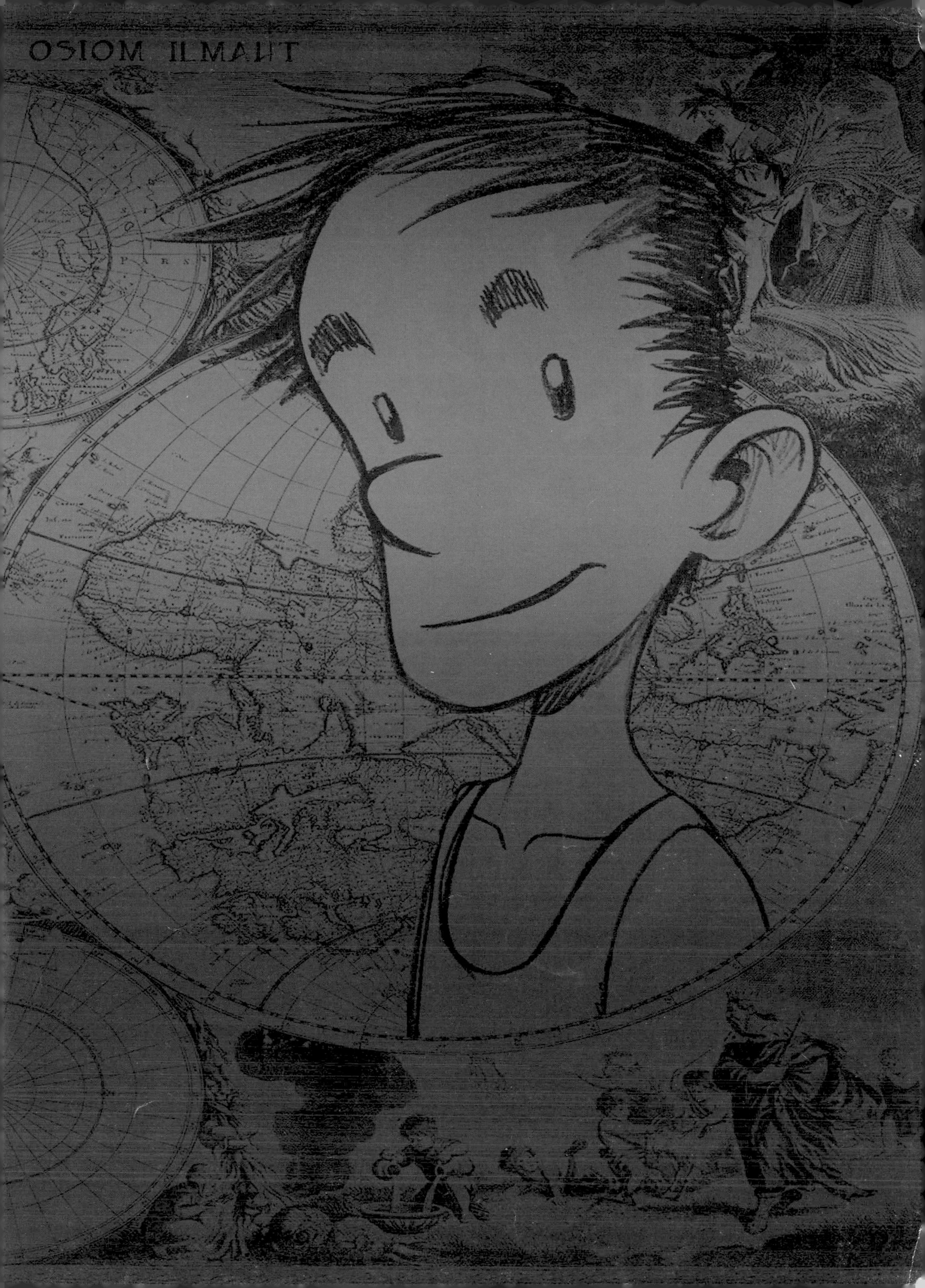
OSIOM ILMAHT

the ElseWhere CHRONICLES

BOOK ONE
THE SHADOW DOOR

ART	STORY	COLORS
BANNISTER	NYKKO	JAFFRÉ

GRAPHIC UNIVERSE™ · MINNEAPOLIS · NEW YORK

To SAbiNe, Léo, ANd Noé
—Nykko

FoR FloRA, thANk you foR youR
psychological ANd culiNARy support.
—BANNiSteR

To MAthiLde
—Jaffré

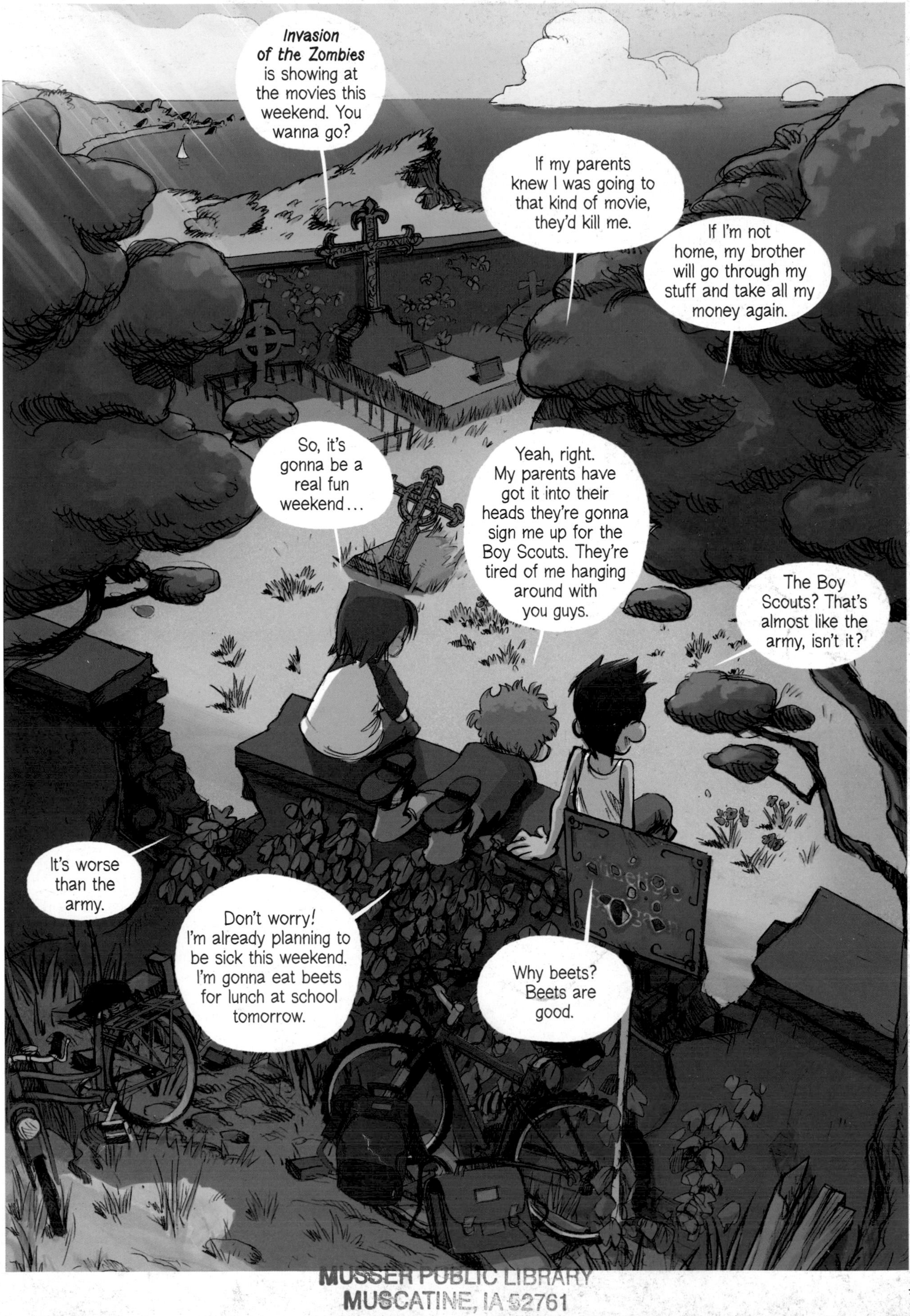

Invasion of the Zombies is showing at the movies this weekend. You wanna go?
If my parents knew I was going to that kind of movie, they'd kill me.
If I'm not home, my brother will go through my stuff and take all my money again.
So, it's gonna be a real fun weekend...
Yeah, right. My parents have got it into their heads they're gonna sign me up for the Boy Scouts. They're tired of me hanging around with you guys.
The Boy Scouts? That's almost like the army, isn't it?
It's worse than the army.
Don't worry! I'm already planning to be sick this weekend. I'm gonna eat beets for lunch at school tomorrow.
Why beets? Beets are good.

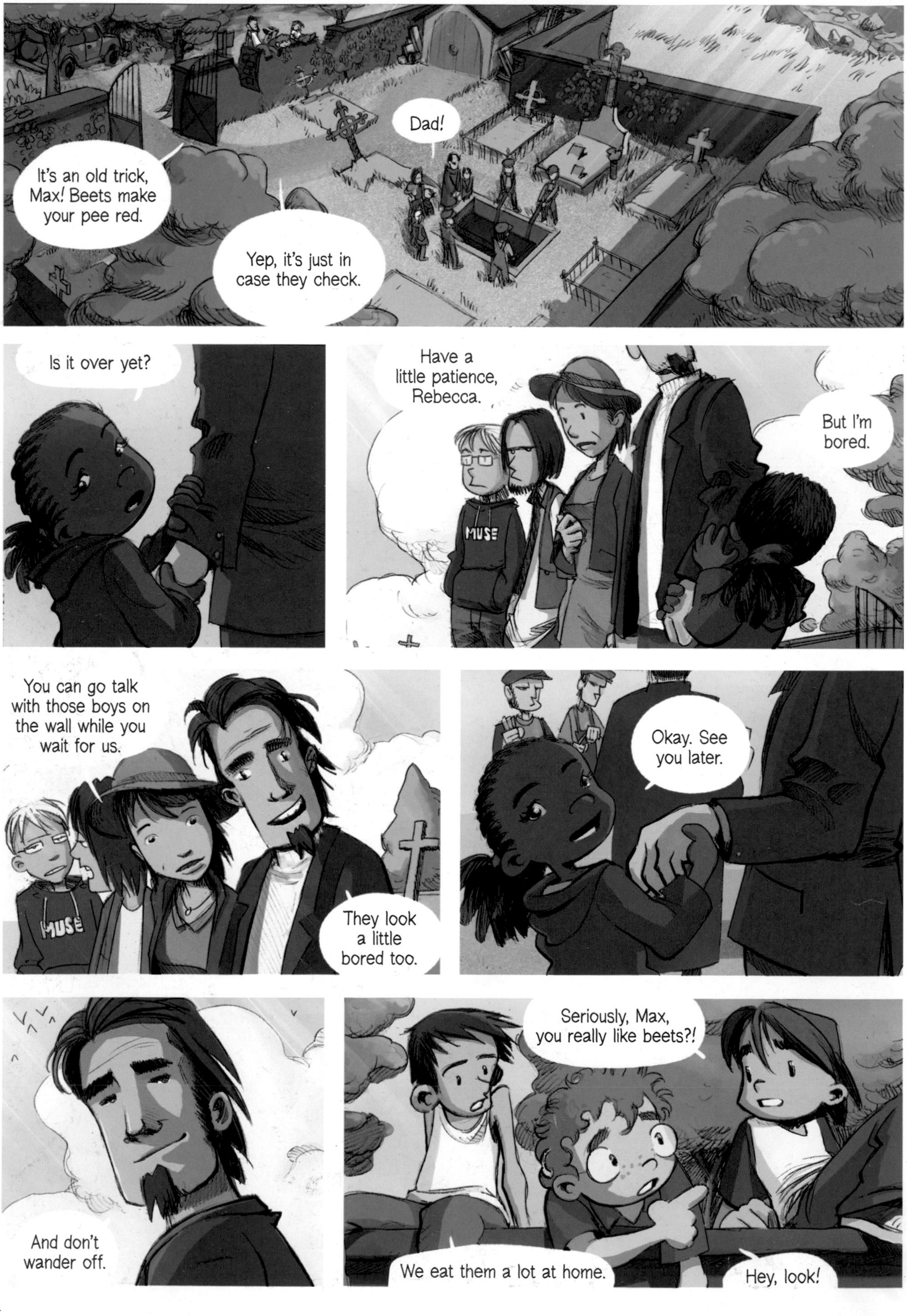
Dad!
It's an old trick, Max! Beets make your pee red.
Yep, it's just in case they check.
Is it over yet?
Have a little patience, Rebecca.
But I'm bored.
You can go talk with those boys on the wall while you wait for us.
They look a little bored too.
Okay. See you later.
And don't wander off.
Seriously, Max, you really like beets?!
We eat them a lot at home.
Hey, look!

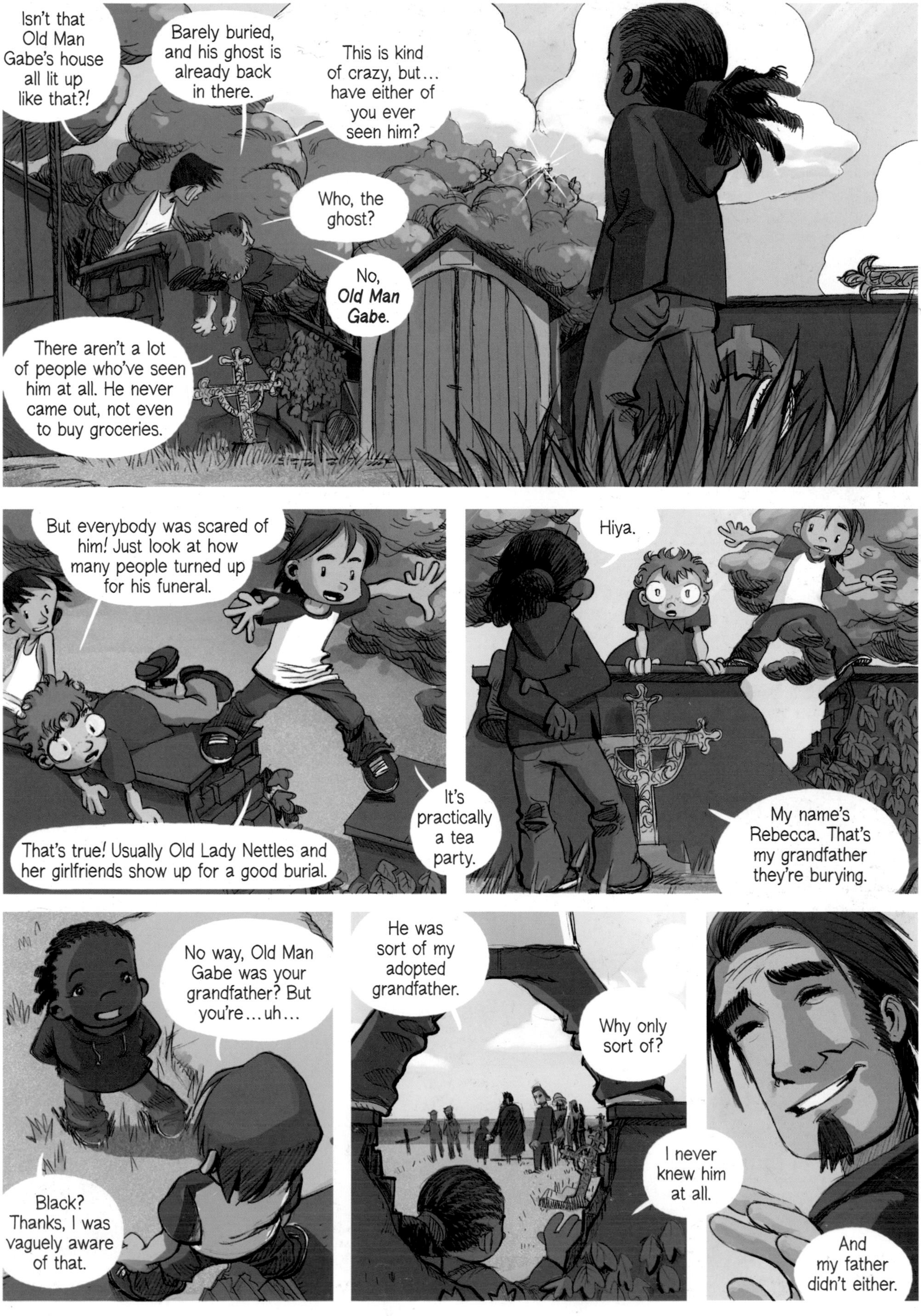
Isn't that Old Man Gabe's house all lit up like that?!
Barely buried, and his ghost is already back in there.
This is kind of crazy, but... have either of you ever seen him?
Who, the ghost?
No, Old Man Gabe.
There aren't a lot of people who've seen him at all. He never came out, not even to buy groceries.
But everybody was scared of him! Just look at how many people turned up for his funeral.
That's true! Usually Old Lady Nettles and her girlfriends show up for a good burial.
It's practically a tea party.
Hiya.
My name's Rebecca. That's my grandfather they're burying.
No way, Old Man Gabe was your grandfather? But you're...uh...
Black? Thanks, I was vaguely aware of that.
He was sort of my adopted grandfather.
Why only sort of?
I never knew him at all.
And my father didn't either.

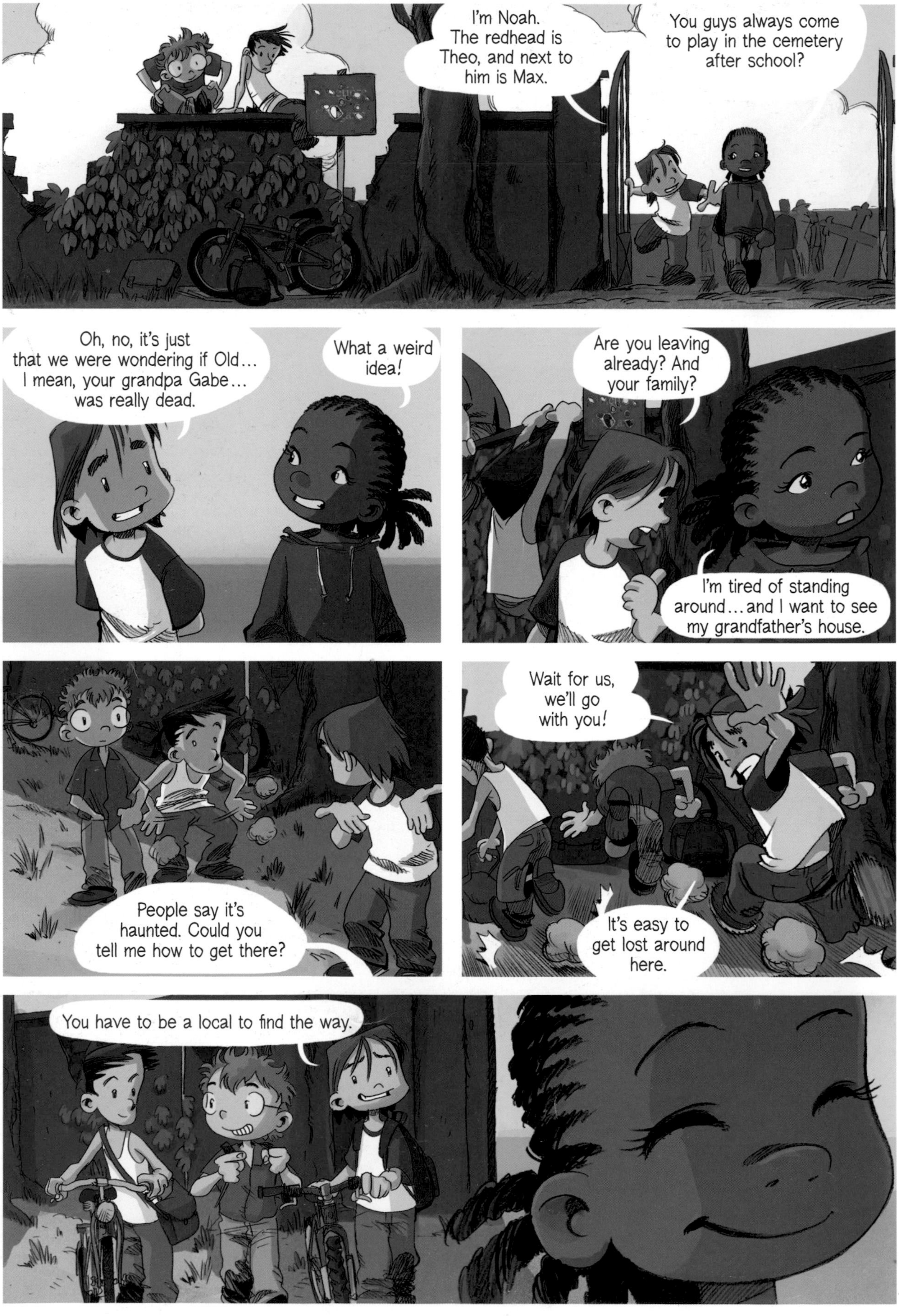
I'm Noah. The redhead is Theo, and next to him is Max.
You guys always come to play in the cemetery after school?
Oh, no, it's just that we were wondering if Old... I mean, your grandpa Gabe... was really dead.
What a weird idea!
Are you leaving already? And your family?
I'm tired of standing around...and I want to see my grandfather's house.
People say it's haunted. Could you tell me how to get there?
Wait for us, we'll go with you!
It's easy to get lost around here.
You have to be a local to find the way.

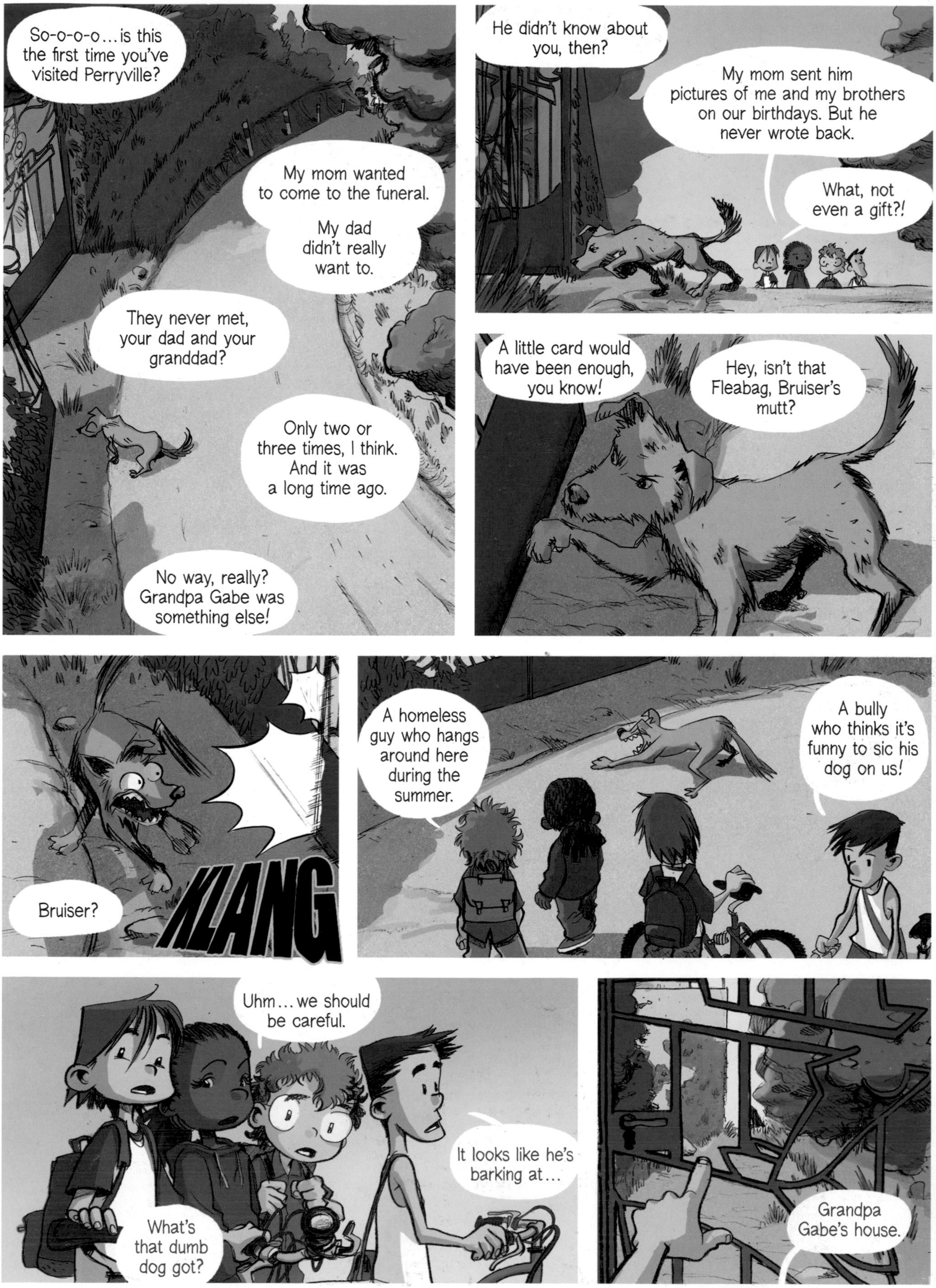
So-o-o-o… is this the first time you've visited Perryville?
My mom wanted to come to the funeral.
My dad didn't really want to.
They never met, your dad and your granddad?
Only two or three times, I think. And it was a long time ago.
No way, really? Grandpa Gabe was something else!
He didn't know about you, then?
My mom sent him pictures of me and my brothers on our birthdays. But he never wrote back.
What, not even a gift?!
A little card would have been enough, you know!
Hey, isn't that Fleabag, Bruiser's mutt?
Bruiser?
KLANG
A homeless guy who hangs around here during the summer.
A bully who thinks it's funny to sic his dog on us!
Uhm… we should be careful.
What's that dumb dog got?
It looks like he's barking at…
Grandpa Gabe's house.

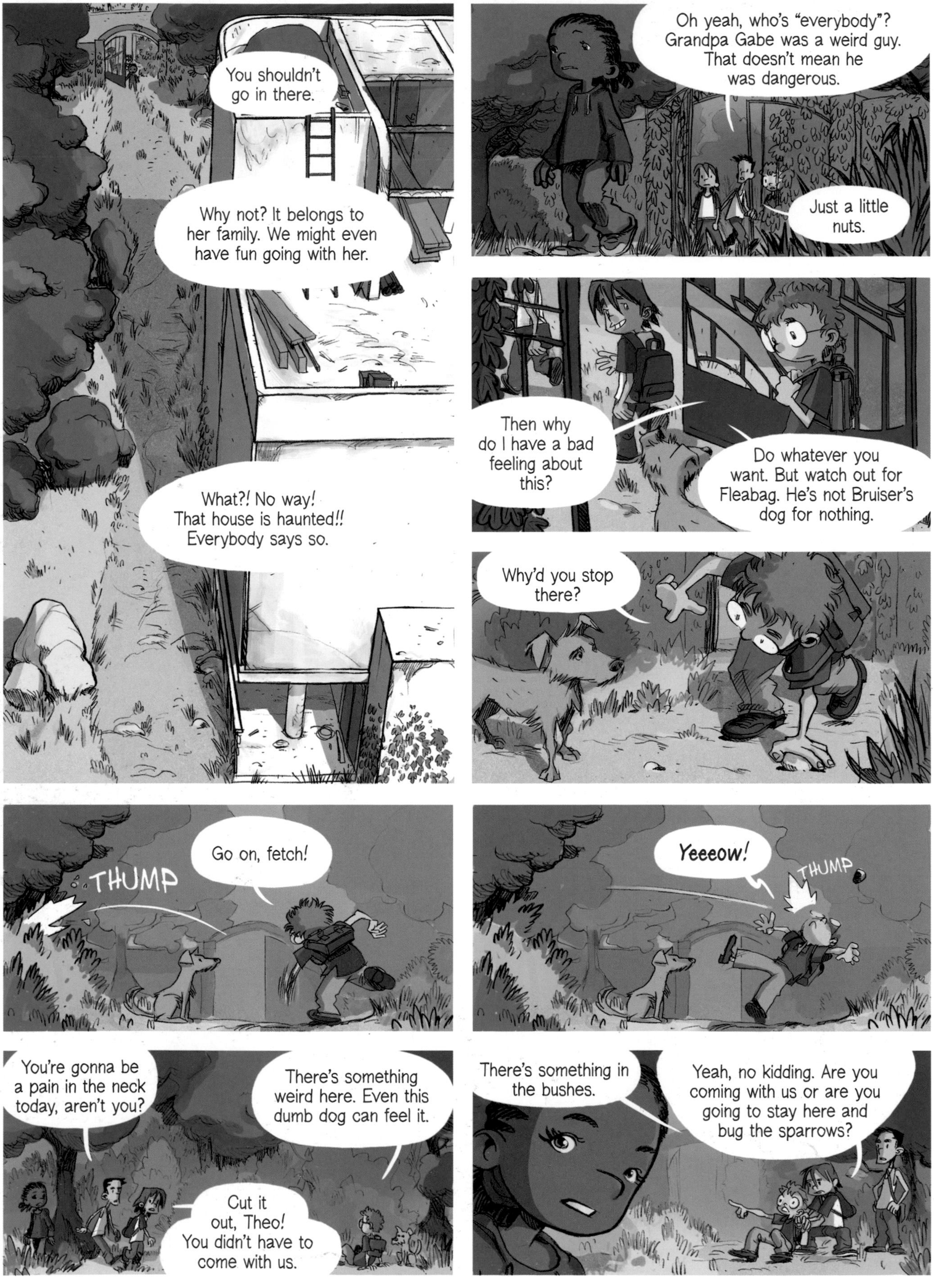

You shouldn't go in there.
Why not? It belongs to her family. We might even have fun going with her.
What?! No way! That house is haunted!! Everybody says so.
Oh yeah, who's "everybody"? Grandpa Gabe was a weird guy. That doesn't mean he was dangerous.
Just a little nuts.
Then why do I have a bad feeling about this?
Do whatever you want. But watch out for Fleabag. He's not Bruiser's dog for nothing.
Why'd you stop there?
THUMP
Go on, fetch!
Yeeeow!
THUMP
You're gonna be a pain in the neck today, aren't you?
There's something weird here. Even this dumb dog can feel it.
Cut it out, Theo! You didn't have to come with us.
There's something in the bushes.
Yeah, no kidding. Are you coming with us or are you going to stay here and bug the sparrows?

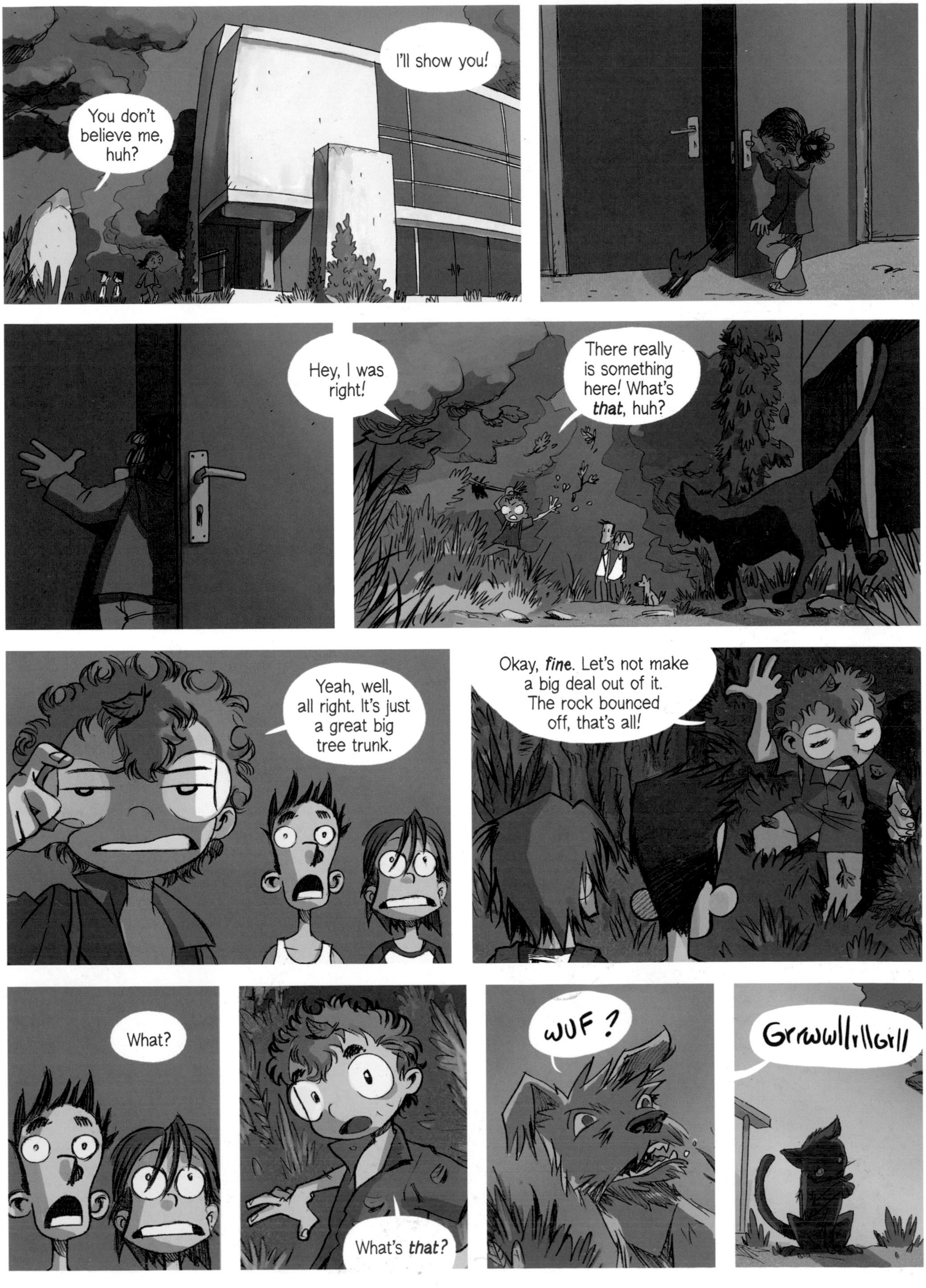
You don't believe me, huh?
I'll show you!
Hey, I was right!
There really is something here! What's *that*, huh?
Yeah, well, all right. It's just a great big tree trunk.
Okay, *fine*. Let's not make a big deal out of it. The rock bounced off, that's all!
What?
What's *that?*
WUF ?
Grwwllrllgrll

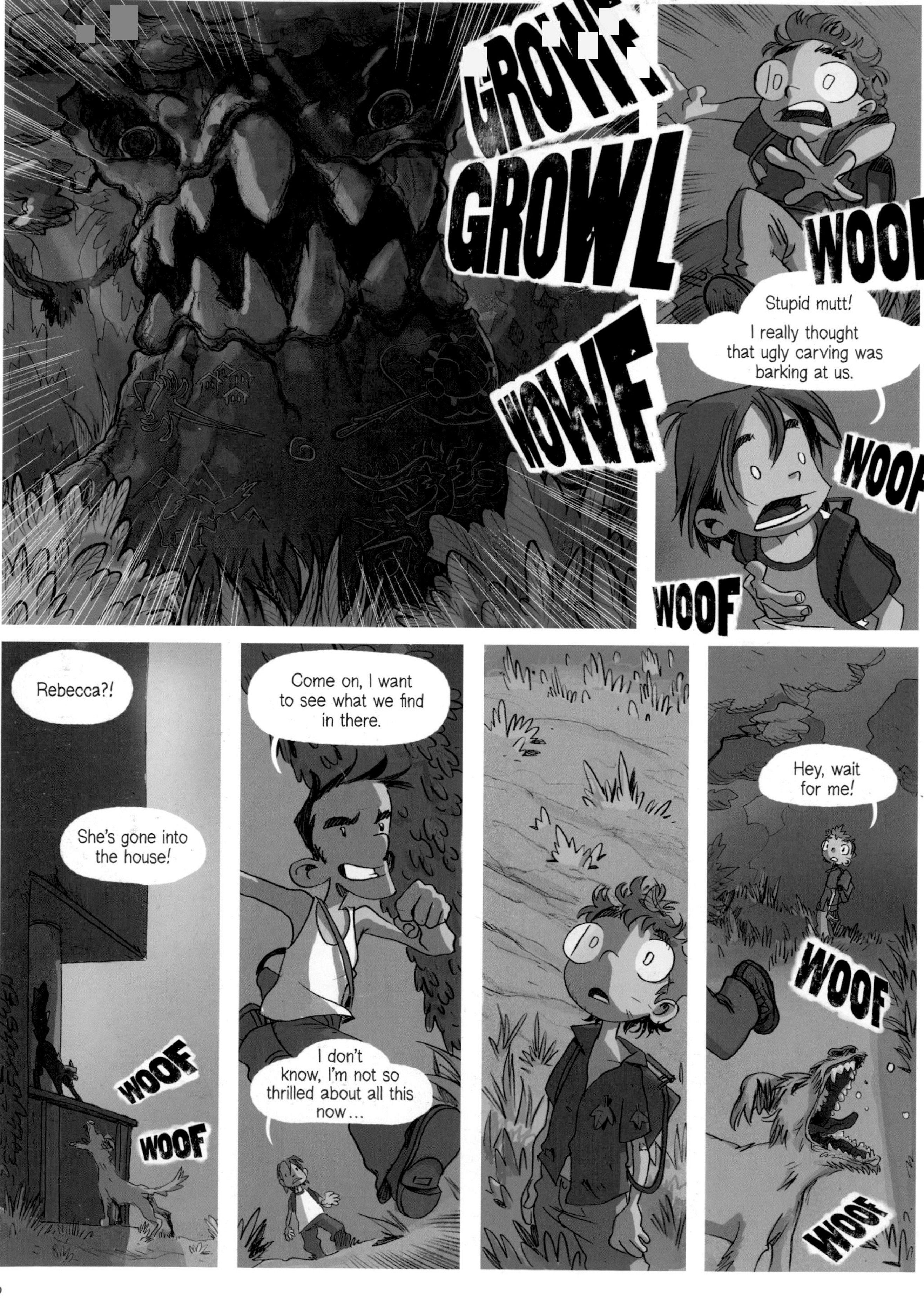
GROWL
GROWL
WOWF
WOOF
Stupid mutt!
I really thought that ugly carving was barking at us.
WOOF
WOOF
Rebecca?!
She's gone into the house!
WOOF
WOOF
Come on, I want to see what we find in there.
I don't know, I'm not so thrilled about all this now...
Hey, wait for me!
WOOF
WOOF

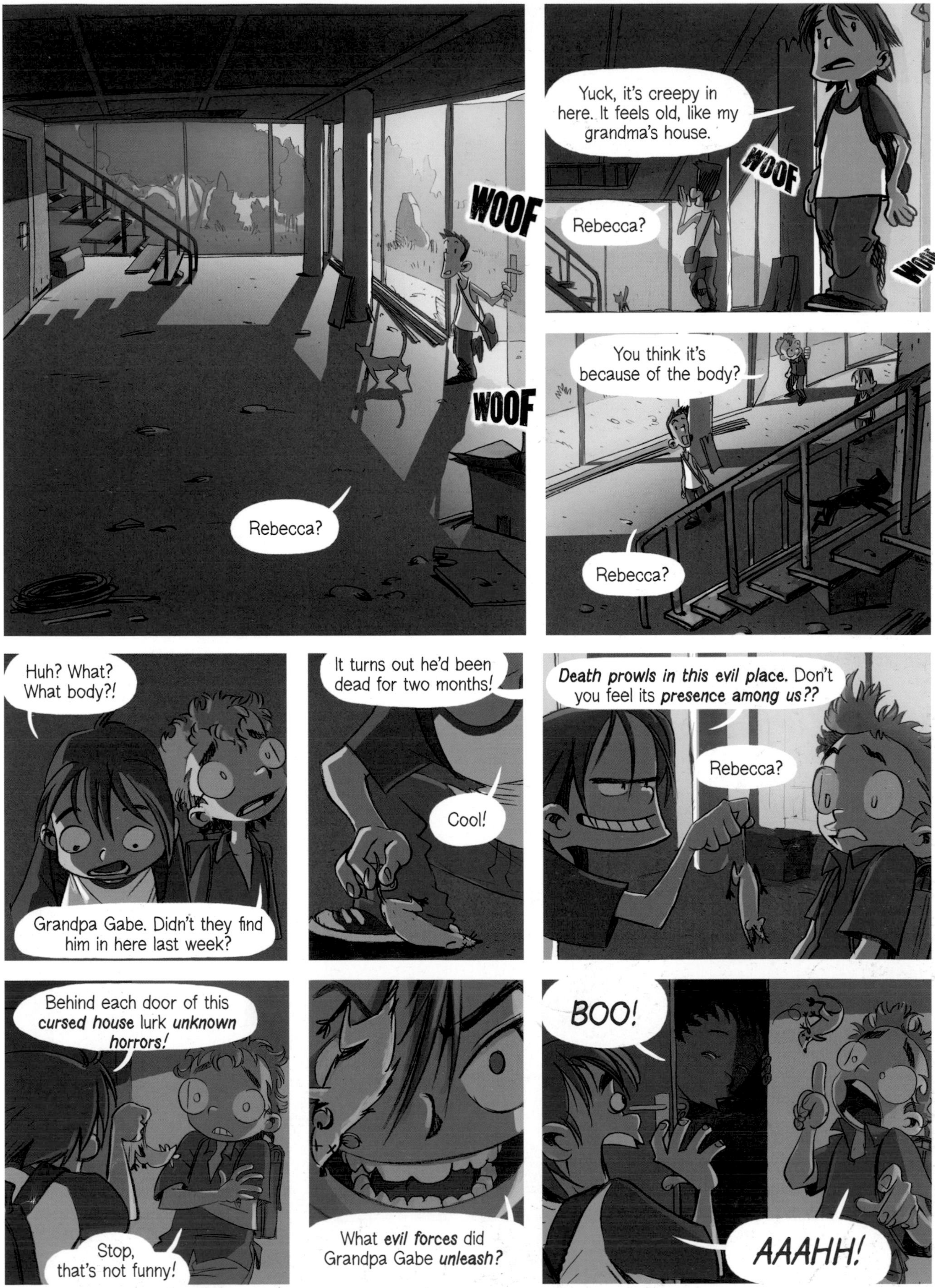
WOOF
WOOF
Rebecca?
Yuck, it's creepy in here. It feels old, like my grandma's house.
WOOF
Rebecca?
WOOF
You think it's because of the body?
Rebecca?
Huh? What? What body?!
Grandpa Gabe. Didn't they find him in here last week?
It turns out he'd been dead for two months!
Cool!
Death prowls in this evil place. Don't you feel its *presence among us??*
Rebecca?
Behind each door of this *cursed house* lurk *unknown horrors!*
Stop, that's not funny!
What *evil forces* did Grandpa Gabe *unleash?*
BOO!
AAAHH!

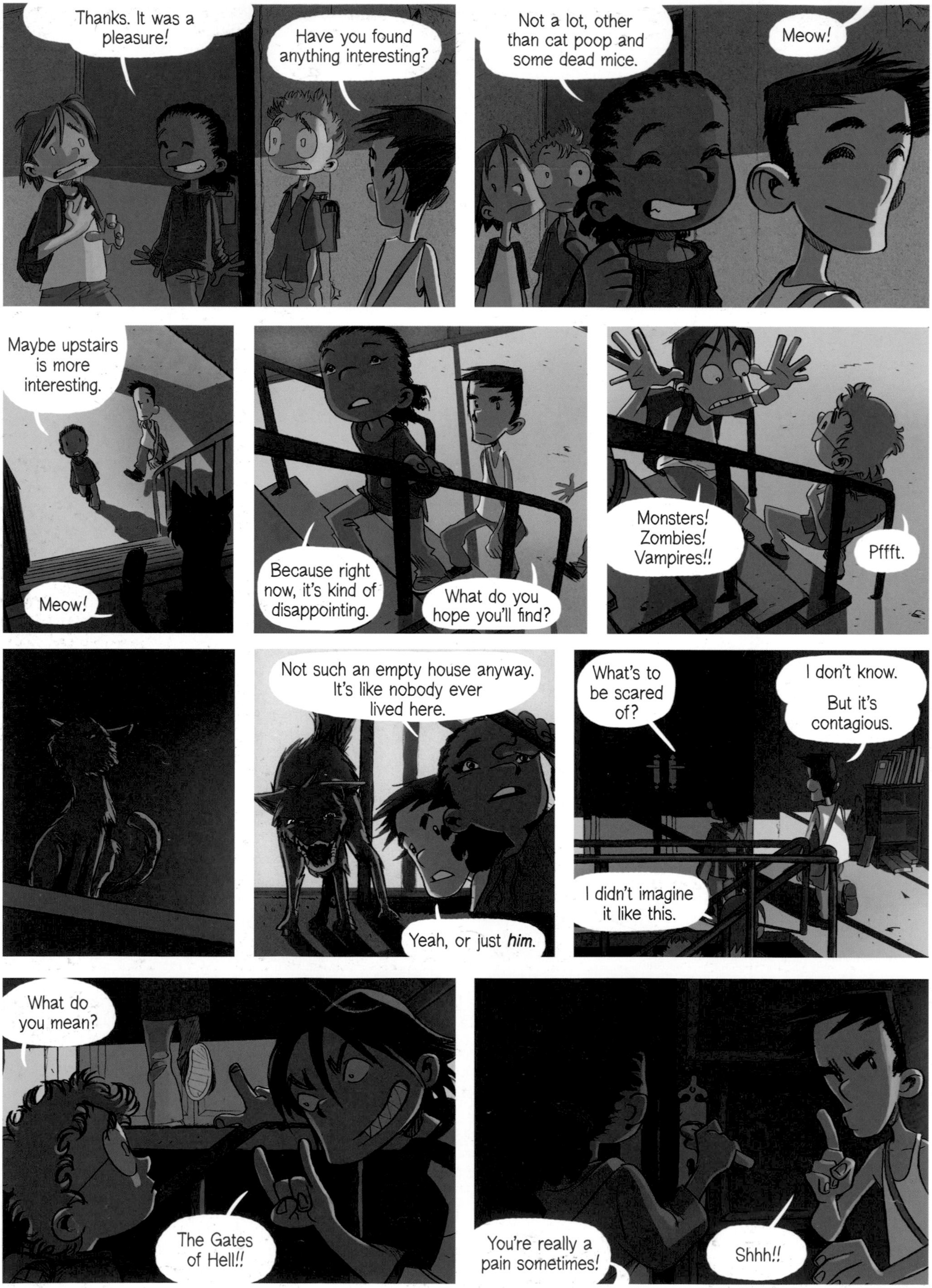
Thanks. It was a pleasure!
Have you found anything interesting?
Not a lot, other than cat poop and some dead mice.
Meow!
Maybe upstairs is more interesting.
Meow!
Because right now, it's kind of disappointing.
What do you hope you'll find?
Monsters! Zombies! Vampires!!
Pffft.
Not such an empty house anyway. It's like nobody ever lived here.
Yeah, or just *him*.
What's to be scared of?
I don't know.
But it's contagious.
I didn't imagine it like this.
What do you mean?
The Gates of Hell!!
You're really a pain sometimes!
Shhh!!

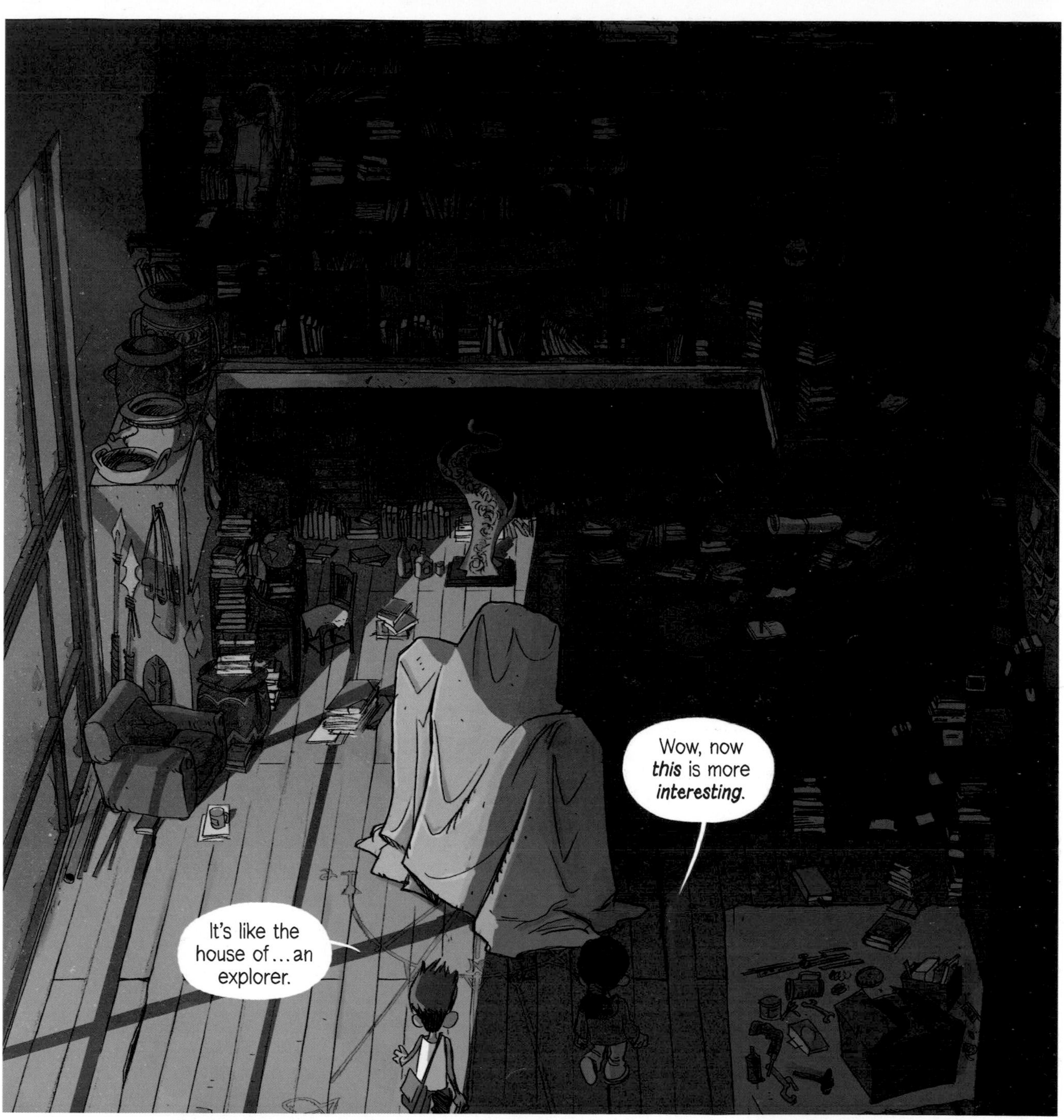
Wow, now *this* is more *interesting*.
It's like the house of…an explorer.

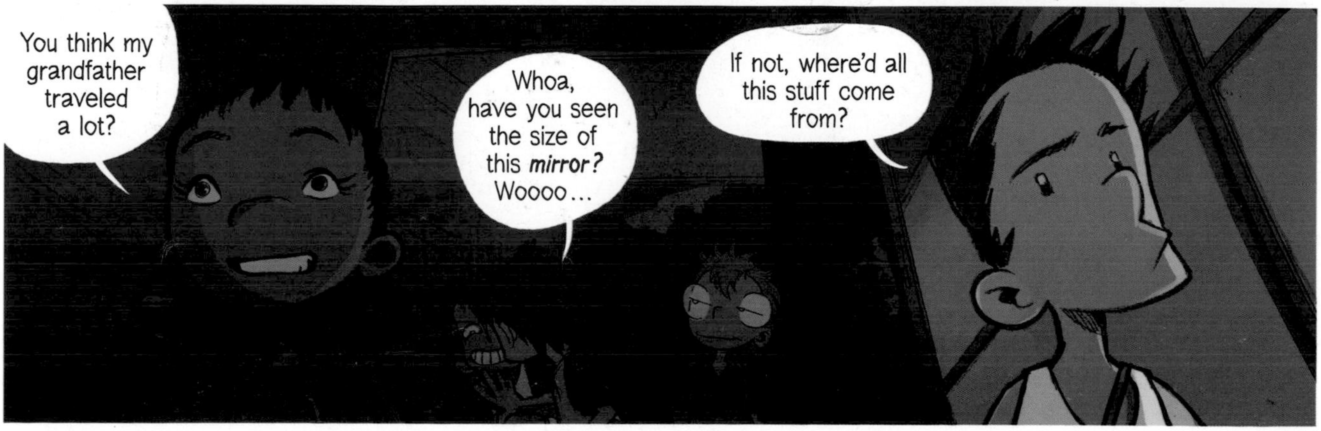
You think my grandfather traveled a lot?
Whoa, have you seen the size of this *mirror?* Woooo…
If not, where'd all this stuff come from?

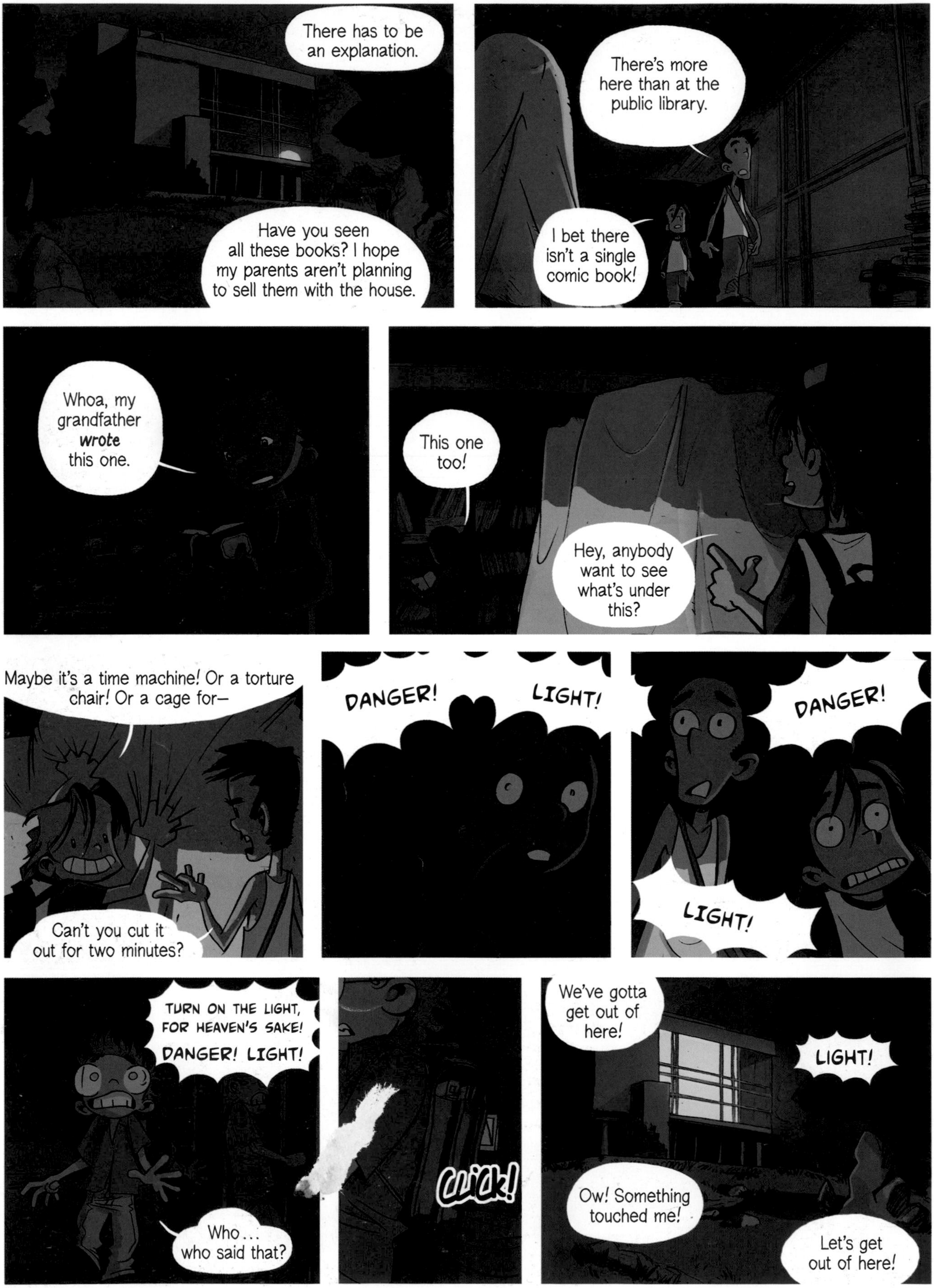
There has to be an explanation.
Have you seen all these books? I hope my parents aren't planning to sell them with the house.
There's more here than at the public library.
I bet there isn't a single comic book!
Whoa, my grandfather **wrote** this one.
This one too!
Hey, anybody want to see what's under this?
Maybe it's a time machine! Or a torture chair! Or a cage for–
Can't you cut it out for two minutes?
DANGER!
LIGHT!
DANGER!
LIGHT!
TURN ON THE LIGHT, FOR HEAVEN'S SAKE!
DANGER! LIGHT!
Who... who said that?
CLICK!
We've gotta get out of here!
LIGHT!
Ow! Something touched me!
Let's get out of here!

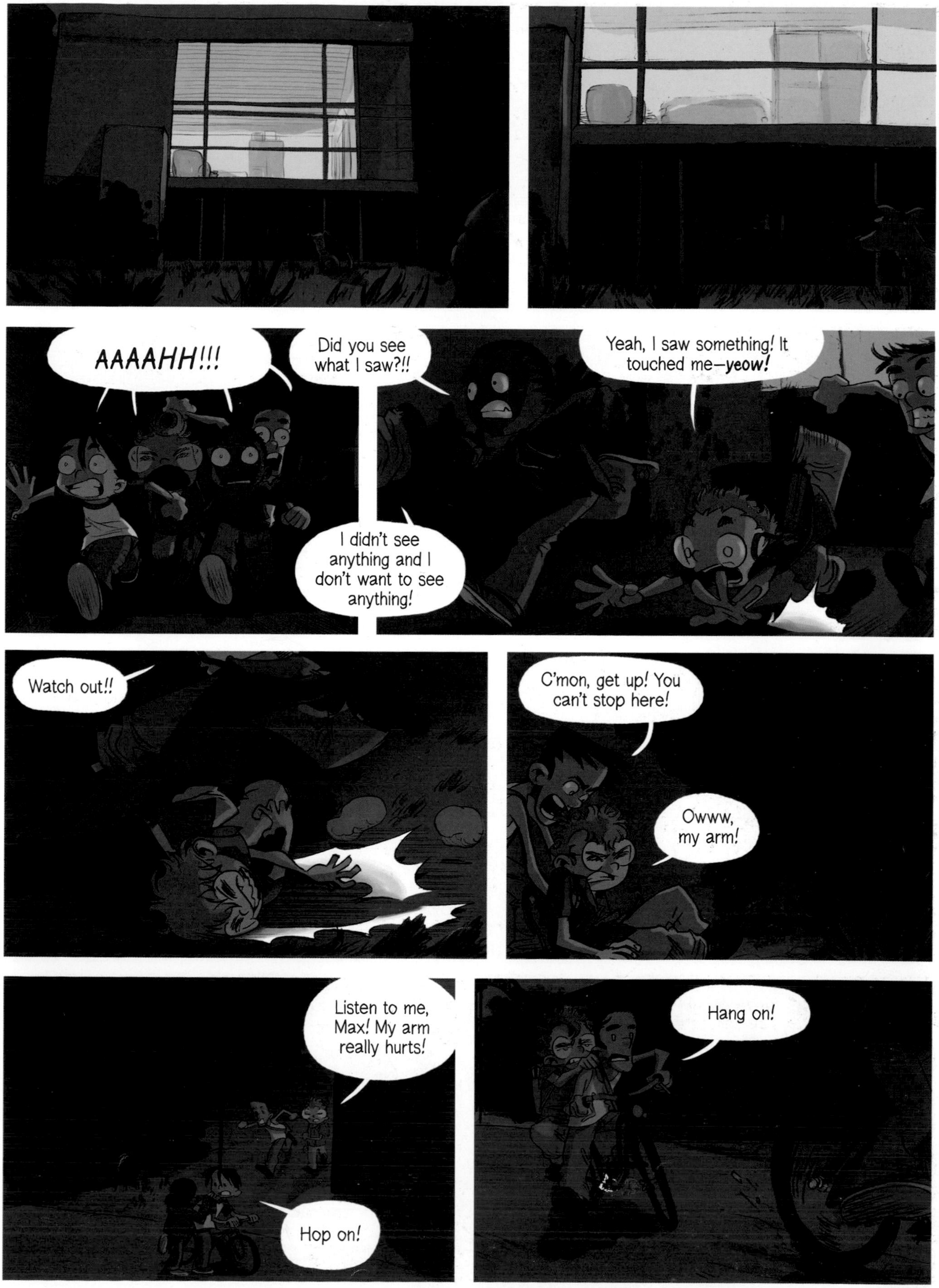
AAAAHH!!!
Did you see what I saw?!!
I didn't see anything and I don't want to see anything!
Yeah, I saw something! It touched me—yeow!
Watch out!!
C'mon, get up! You can't stop here!
Owww, my arm!
Listen to me, Max! My arm really hurts!
Hop on!
Hang on!

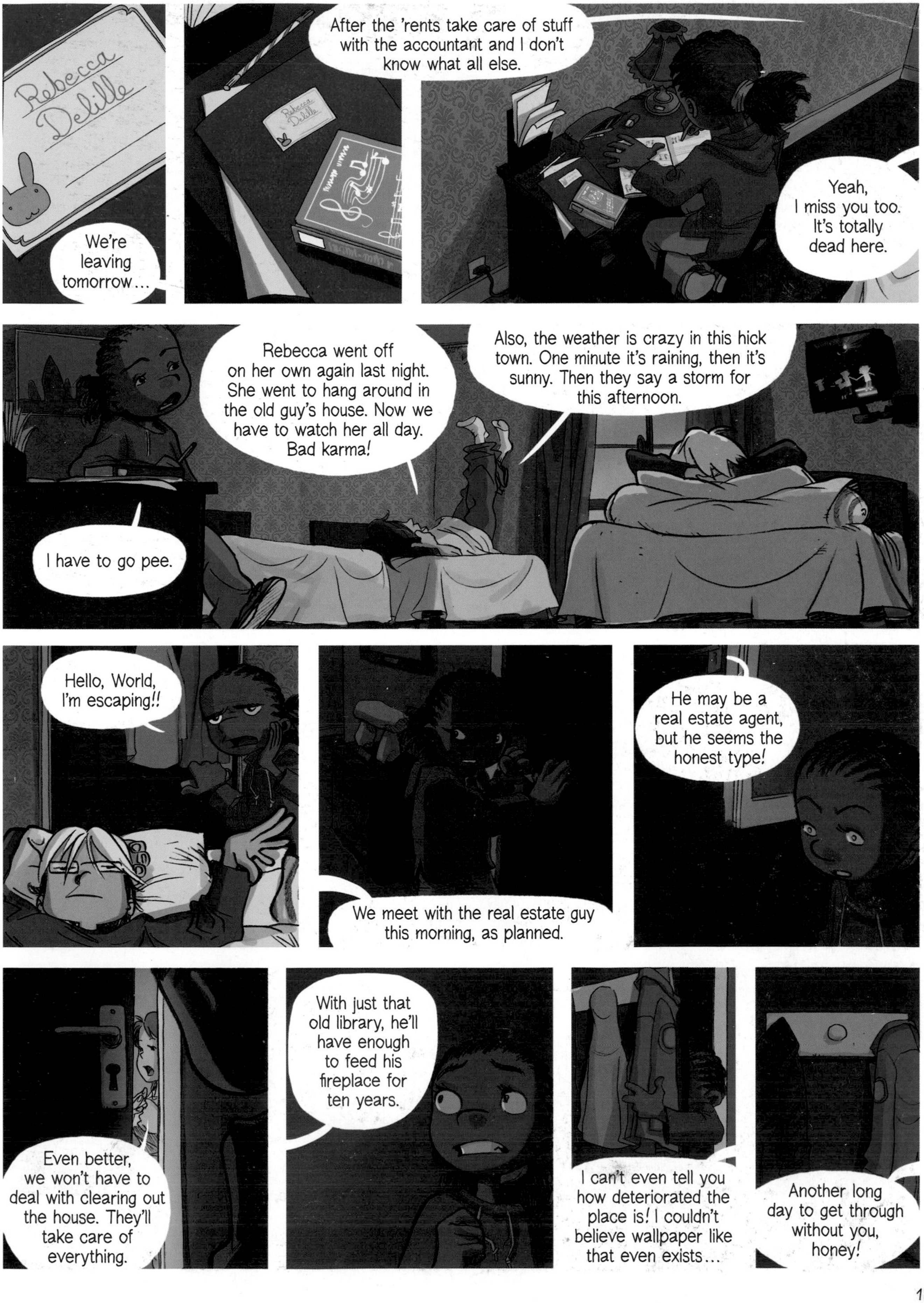

Rebecca Delille
We're leaving tomorrow…
After the 'rents take care of stuff with the accountant and I don't know what all else.
Yeah, I miss you too. It's totally dead here.
Rebecca went off on her own again last night. She went to hang around in the old guy's house. Now we have to watch her all day. Bad karma!
Also, the weather is crazy in this hick town. One minute it's raining, then it's sunny. Then they say a storm for this afternoon.
I have to go pee.
Hello, World, I'm escaping!!
We meet with the real estate guy this morning, as planned.
He may be a real estate agent, but he seems the honest type!
Even better, we won't have to deal with clearing out the house. They'll take care of everything.
With just that old library, he'll have enough to feed his fireplace for ten years.
I can't even tell you how deteriorated the place is! I couldn't believe wallpaper like that even exists…
Another long day to get through without you, honey!

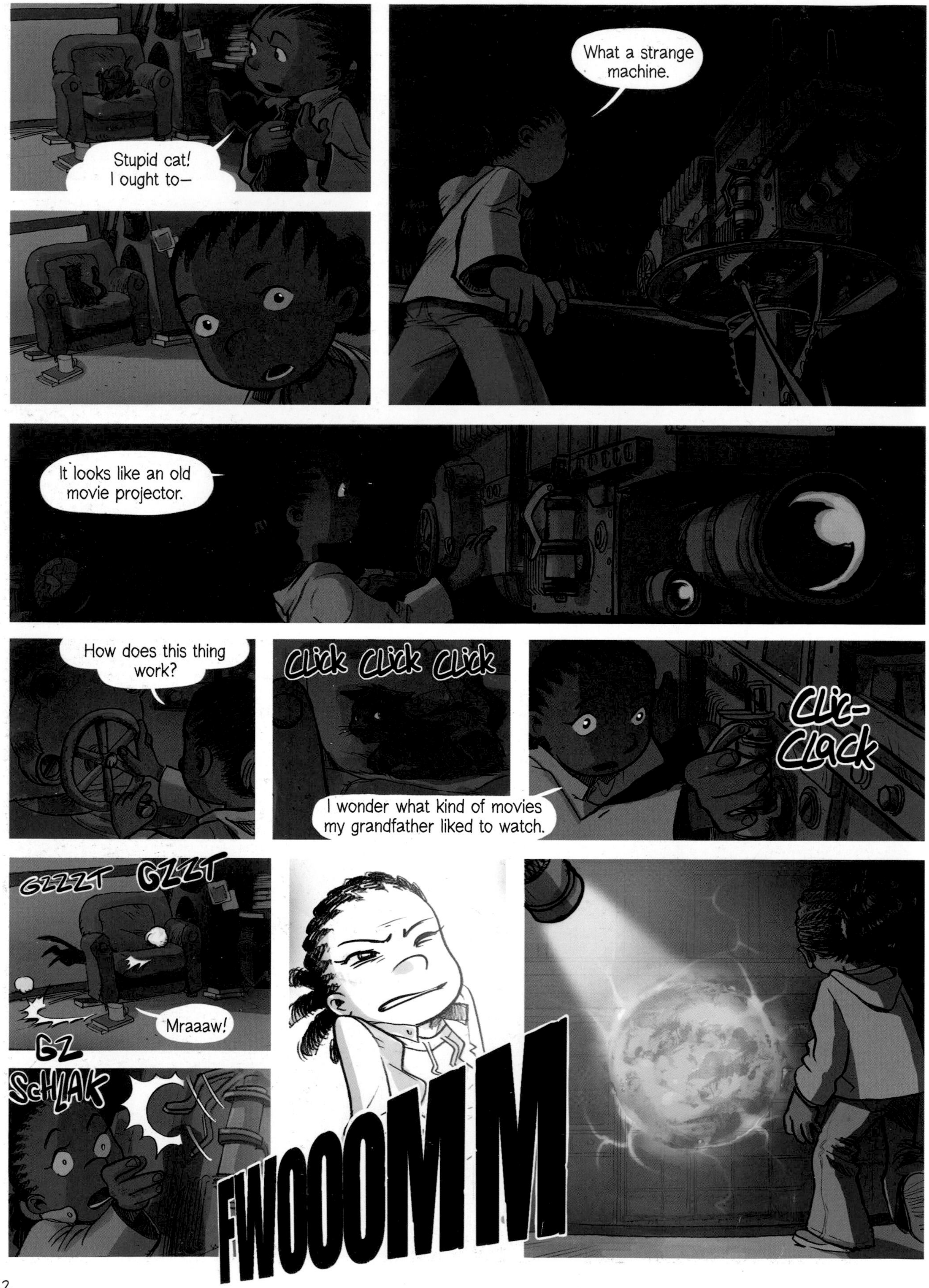
Stupid cat! I ought to—
What a strange machine.
It looks like an old movie projector.
How does this thing work?
CLICK CLICK CLICK
CLIC-CLACK
I wonder what kind of movies my grandfather liked to watch.
GZZZT GZZT
Mraaaw!
GZ
SCHLAK
FWOOOMMM

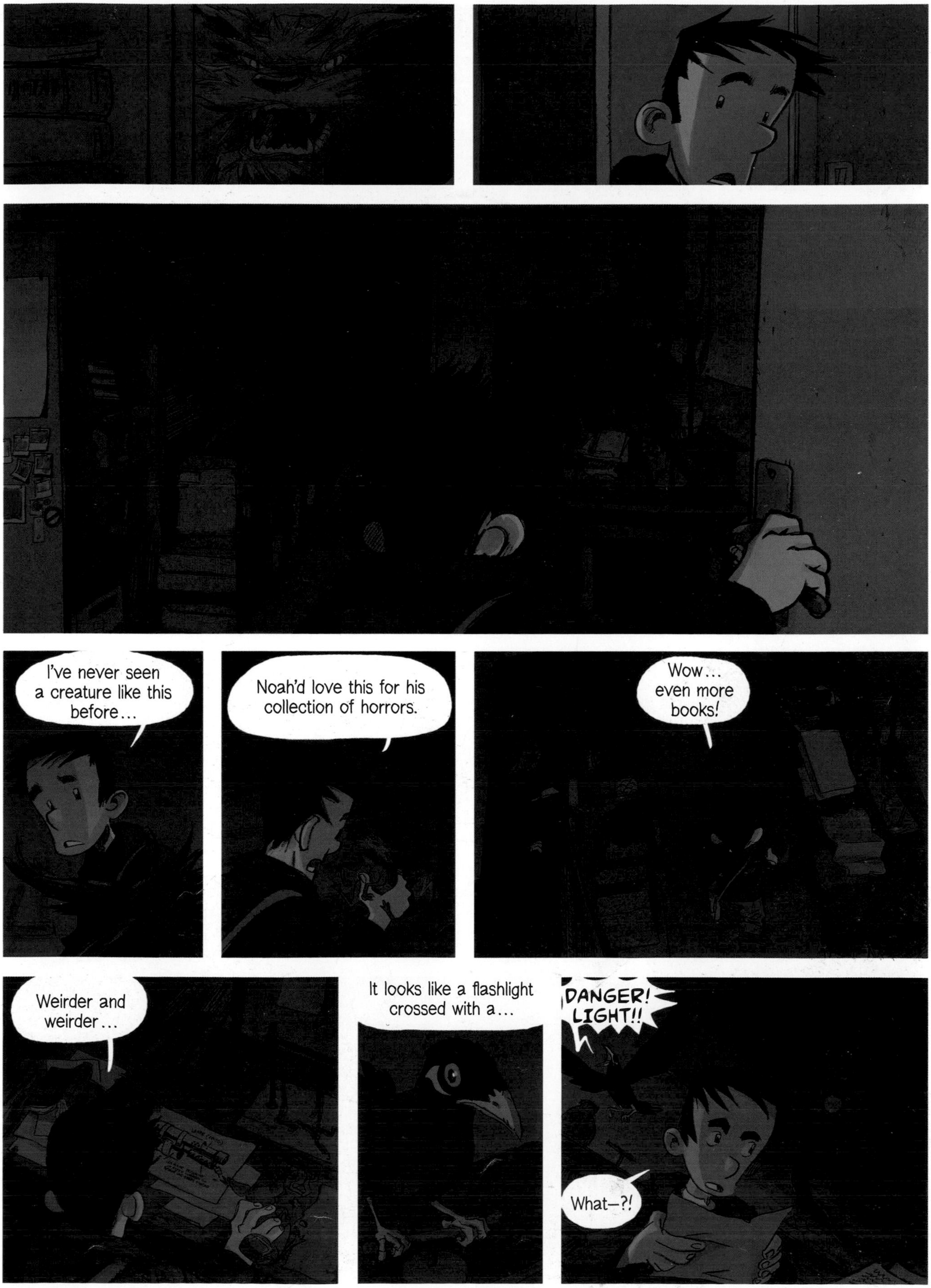

I've never seen a creature like this before...
Noah'd love this for his collection of horrors.
Wow... even more books!
Weirder and weirder...
It looks like a flashlight crossed with a...
DANGER! LIGHT!!
What—?!

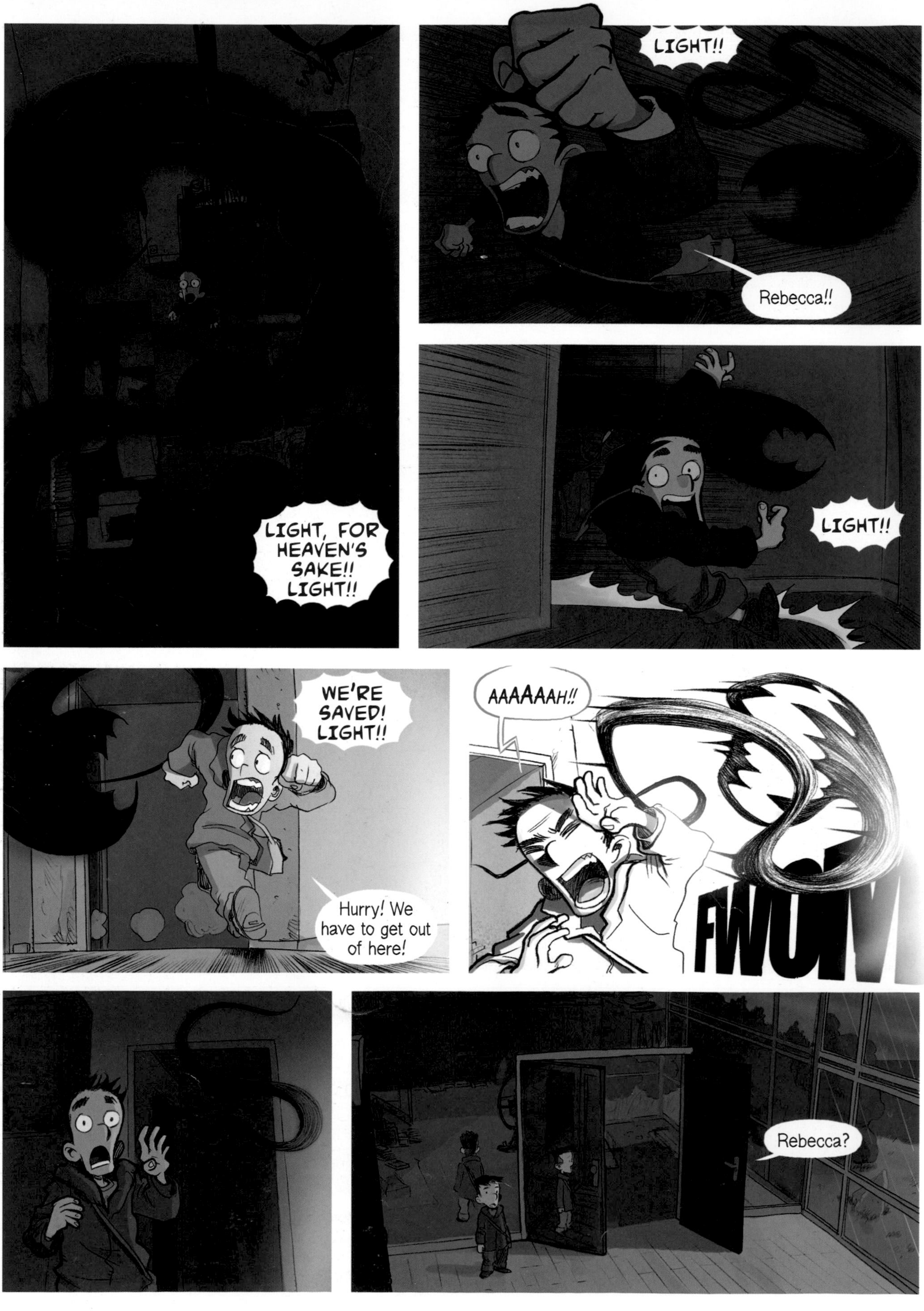
LIGHT, FOR HEAVEN'S SAKE!! LIGHT!!
LIGHT!!
Rebecca!!
LIGHT!!
WE'RE SAVED! LIGHT!!
Hurry! We have to get out of here!
AAAAAAH!!
FWOM
Rebecca?

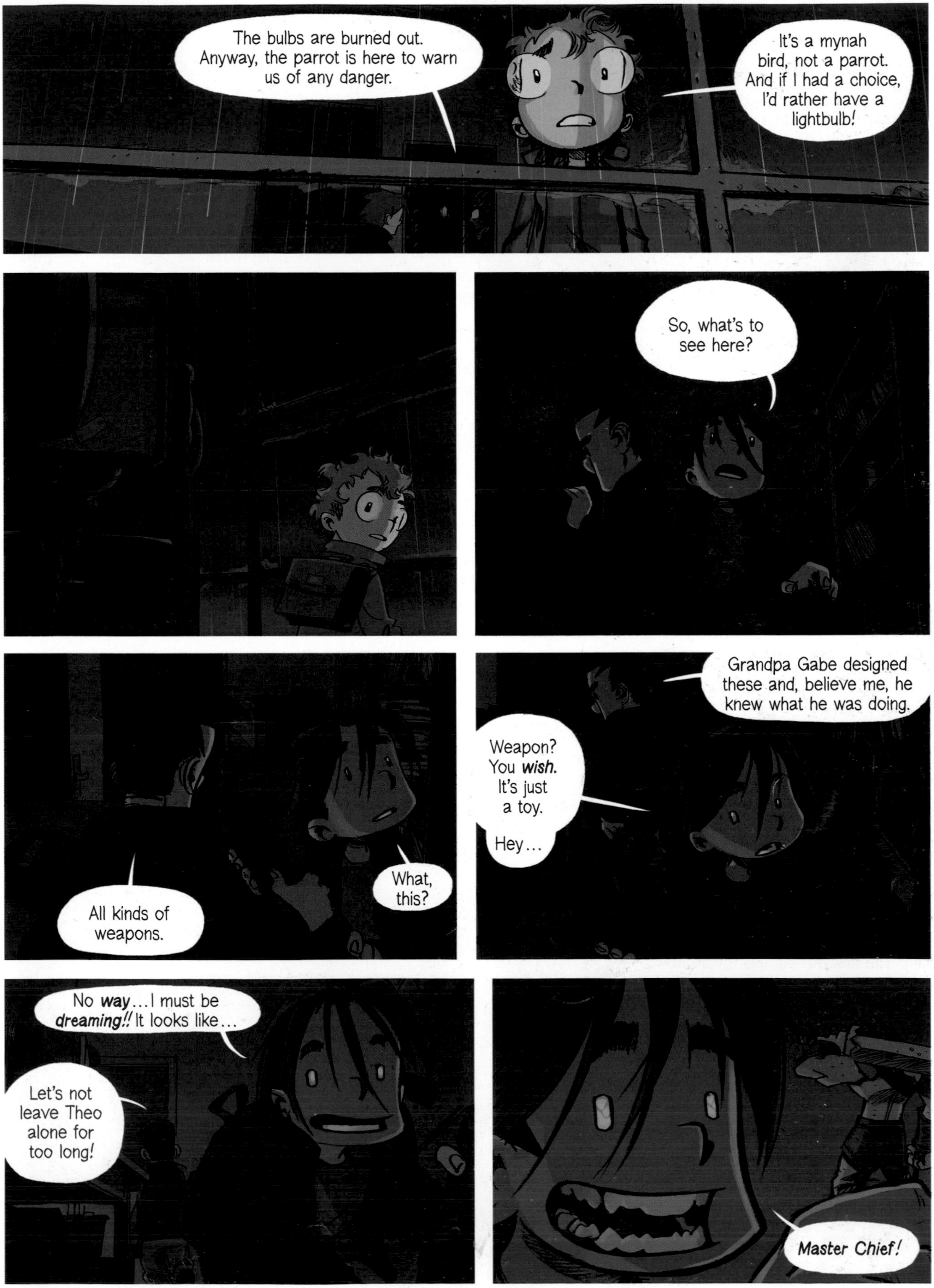

The bulbs are burned out. Anyway, the parrot is here to warn us of any danger.
It's a mynah bird, not a parrot. And if I had a choice, I'd rather have a lightbulb!
So, what's to see here?
All kinds of weapons.
What, this?
Grandpa Gabe designed these and, believe me, he knew what he was doing.
Weapon? You *wish.* It's just a toy.
Hey...
No **way**... I must be ***dreaming!!*** It looks like...
Let's not leave Theo alone for too long!
Master Chief!

28

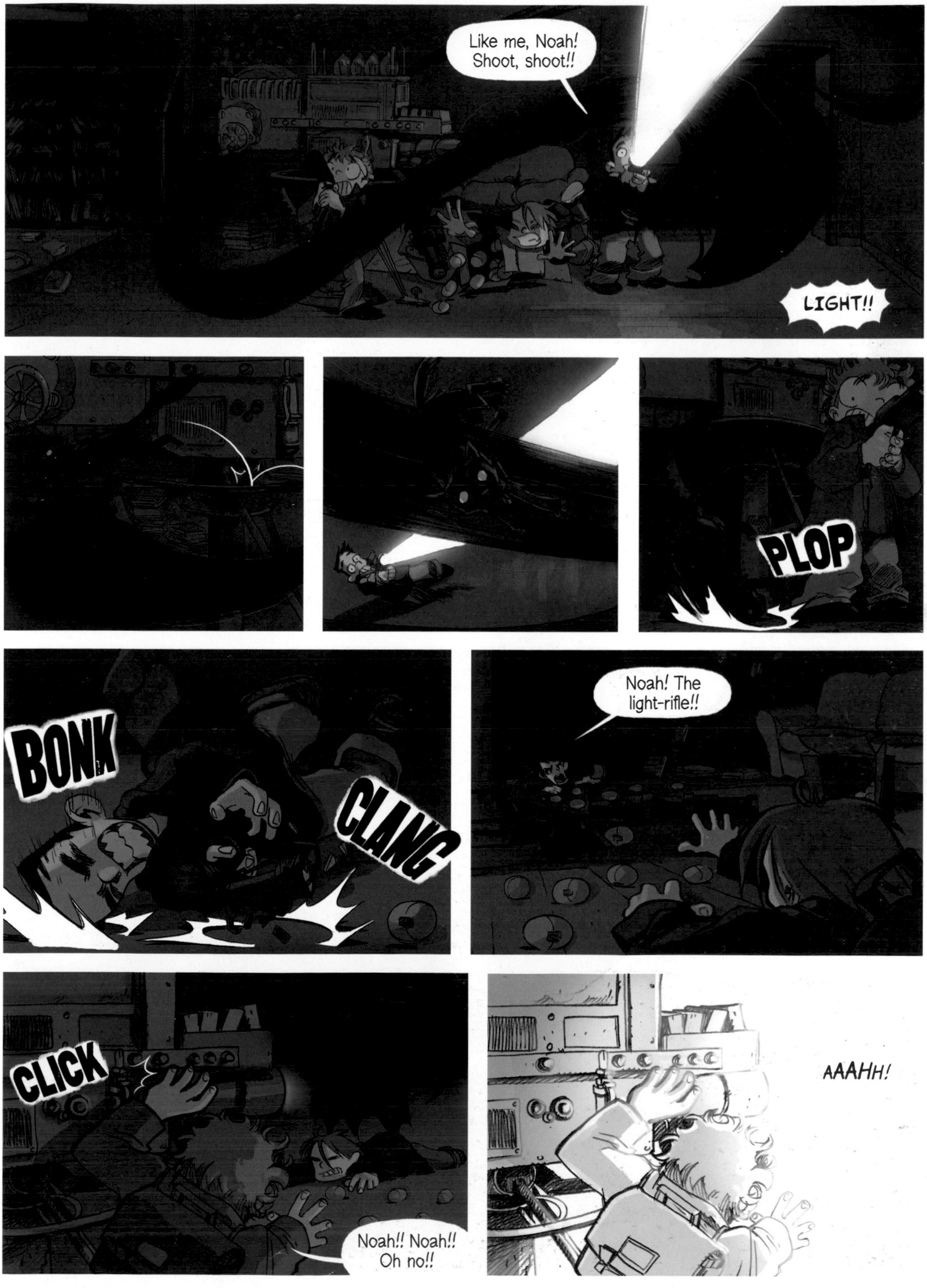
Like me, Noah! Shoot, shoot!!
LIGHT!!
PLOP
BONK
CLANG
Noah! The light-rifle!!
CLICK
Noah!! Noah!! Oh no!!
AAAHH!

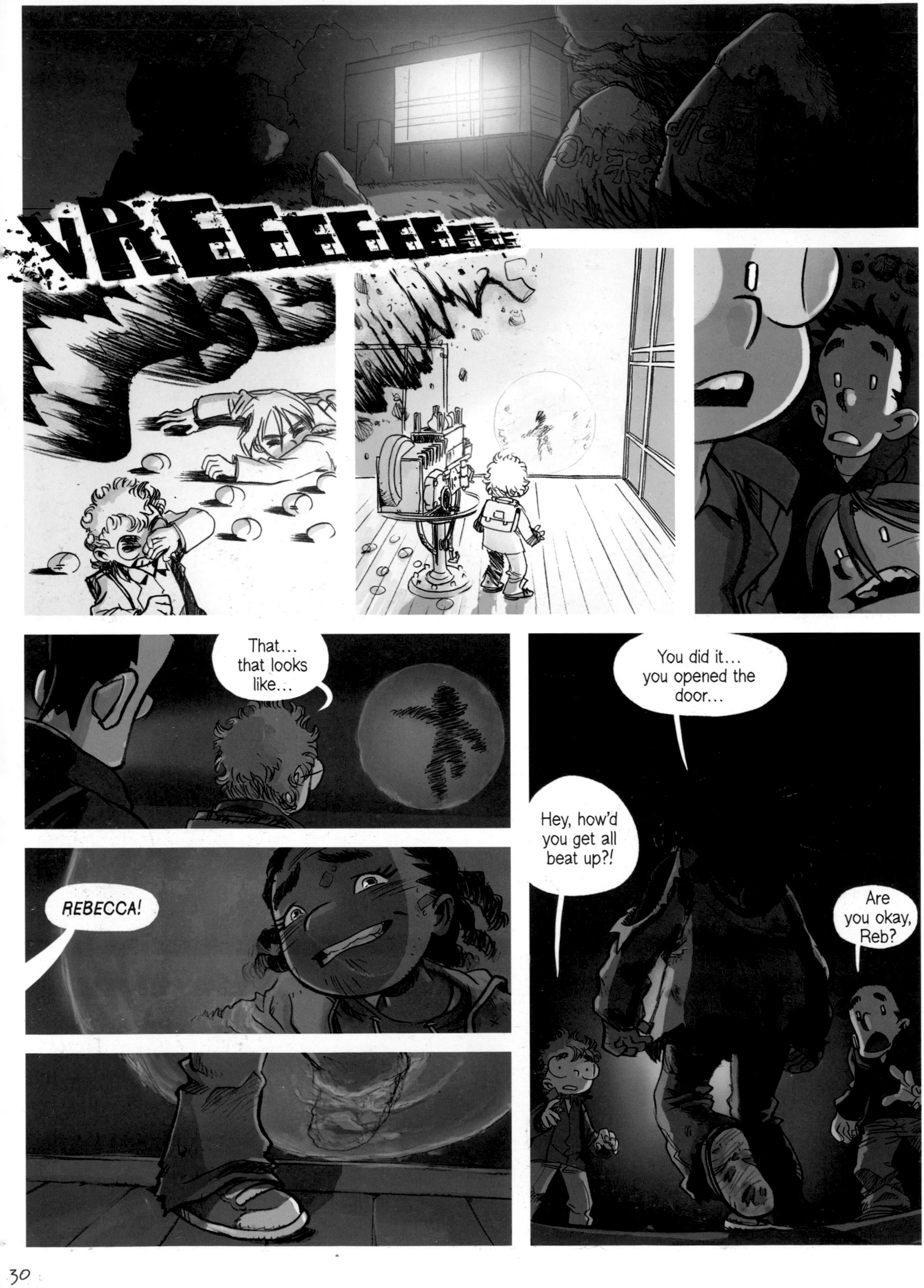
VREEEEEEEEE
That... that looks like...
You did it... you opened the door...
REBECCA!
Hey, how'd you get all beat up?!
Are you okay, Reb?

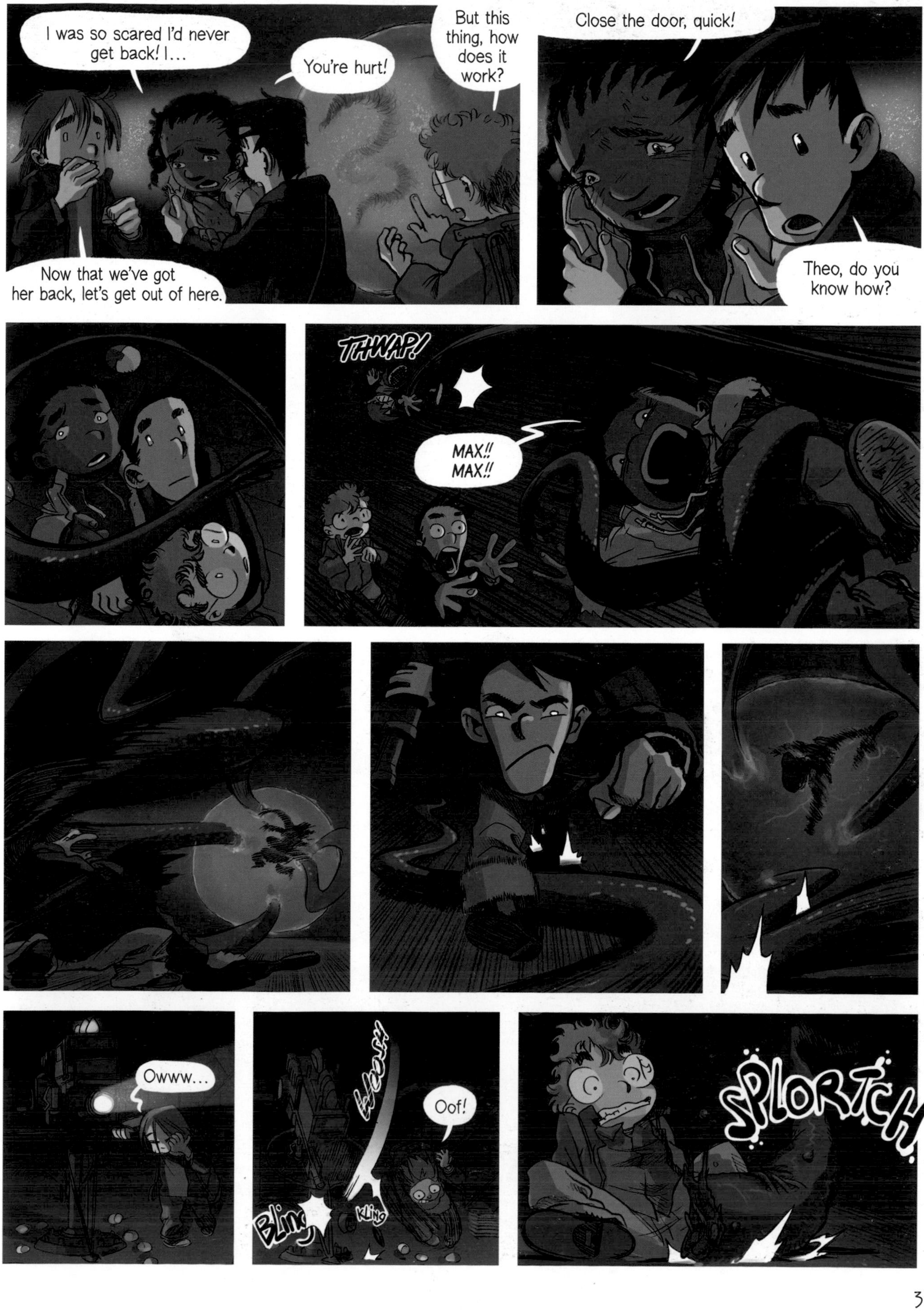
I was so scared I'd never get back! I...
You're hurt!
But this thing, how does it work?
Now that we've got her back, let's get out of here.
Close the door, quick!
Theo, do you know how?
THWAP!
MAX!! MAX!!
Owww...
Oof!
Bling
KLING
SPLORTCH

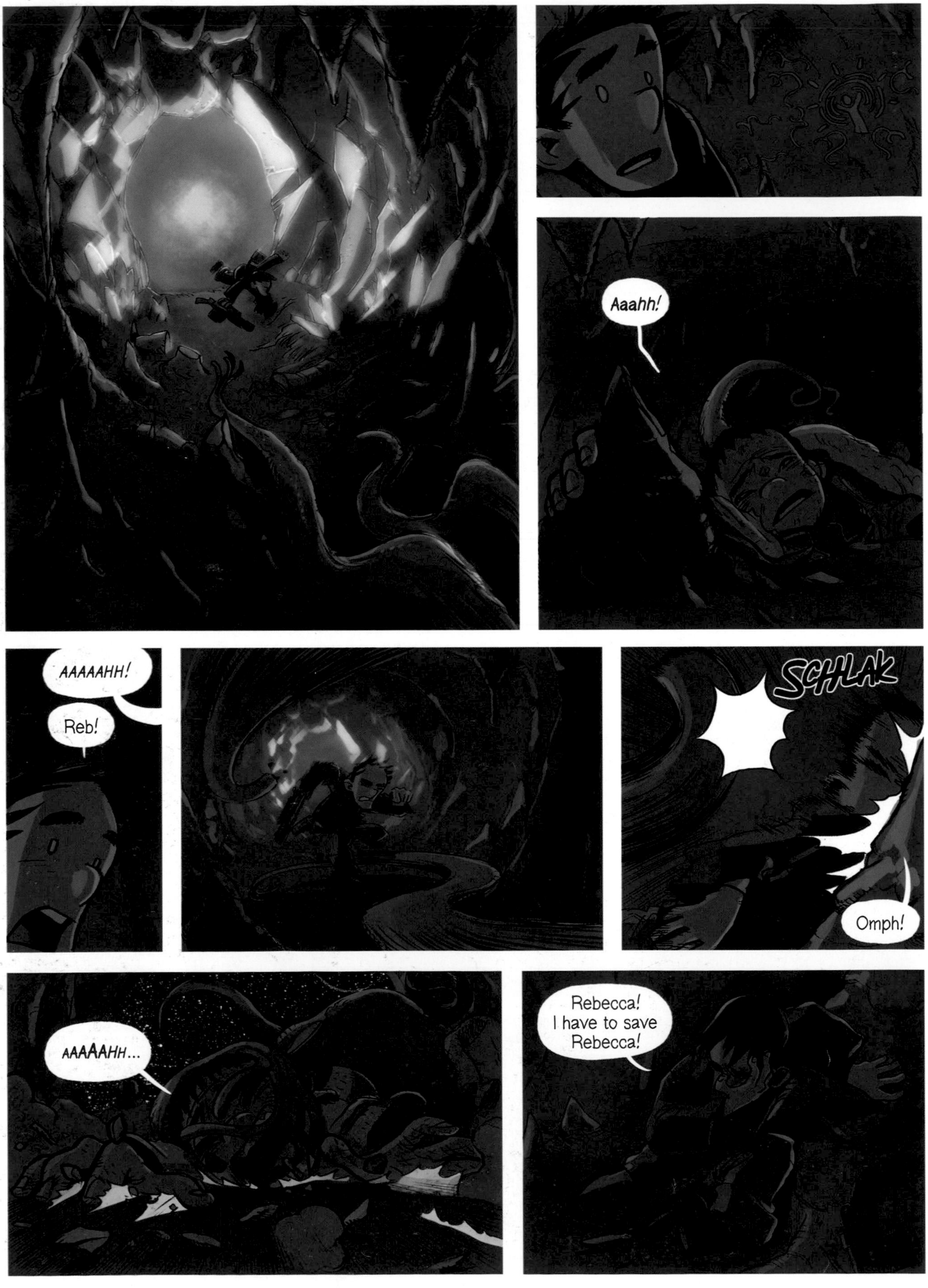
Aaahh!
AAAAAHH!
Reb!
SCHLAK
Omph!
AAAAAHH...
Rebecca!
I have to save
Rebecca!

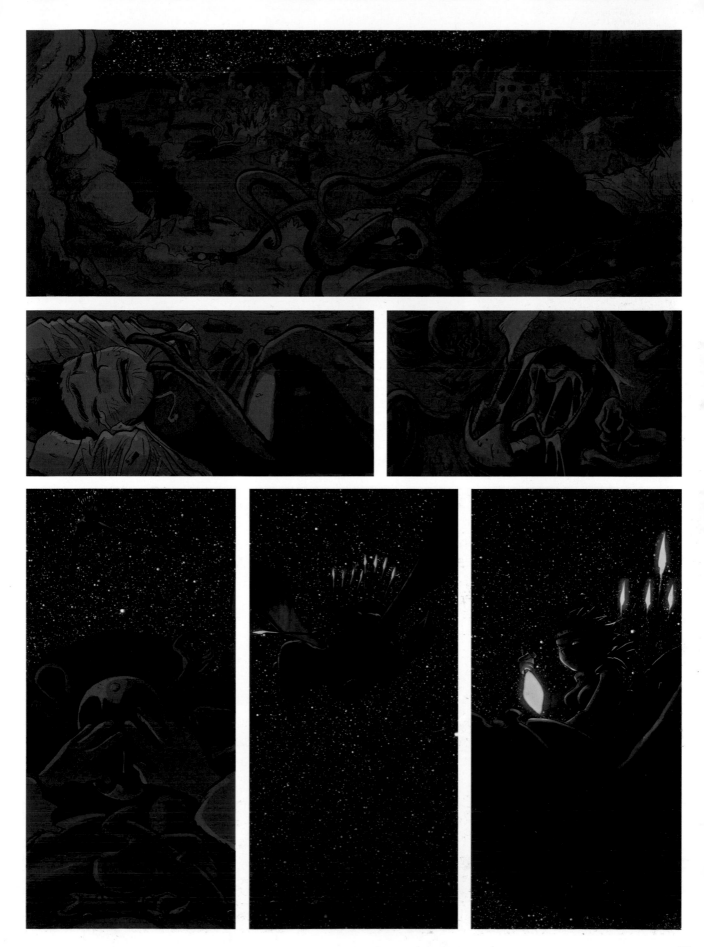

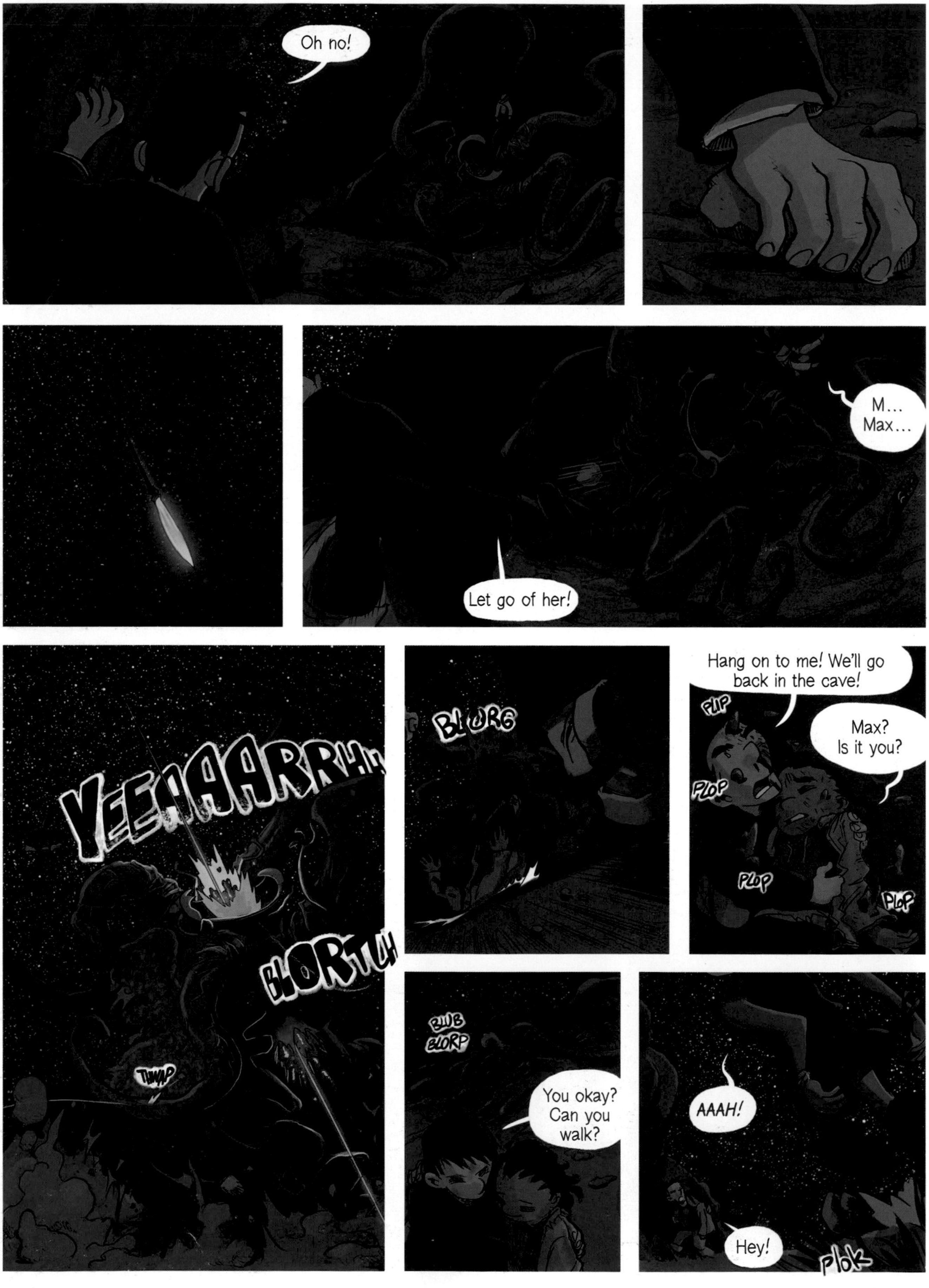
Oh no!
M... Max...
Let go of her!
YEEAAARRH!!
BLORTCH
THWAP
BLORG
Hang on to me! We'll go back in the cave!
PLIP
Max? Is it you?
PLOP
PLOP
PLOP
BLUB BLORP
You okay? Can you walk?
AAAH!
Hey!
Plok

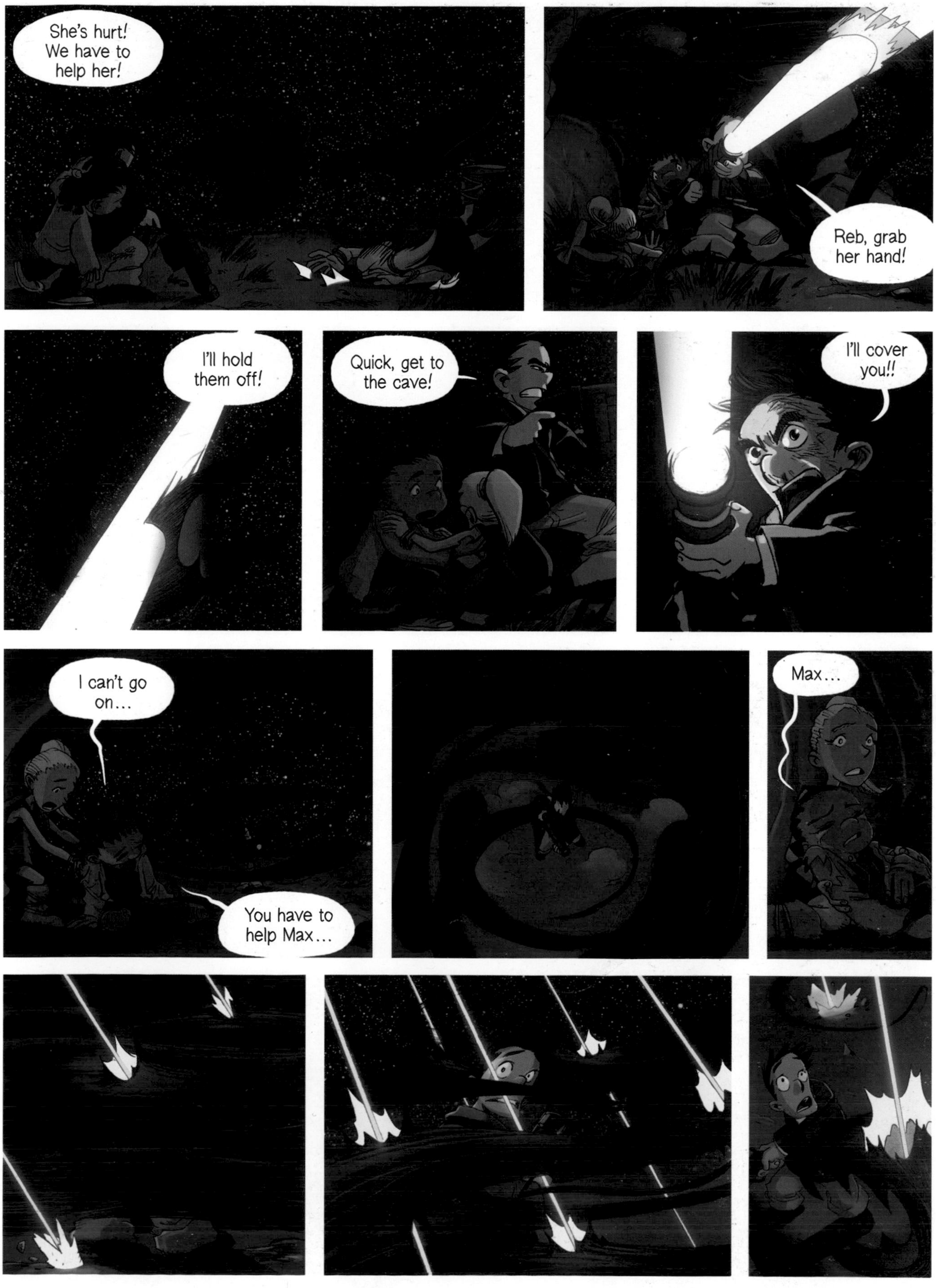
She's hurt! We have to help her!
Reb, grab her hand!
I'll hold them off!
Quick, get to the cave!
I'll cover you!!
I can't go on...
You have to help Max...
Max...

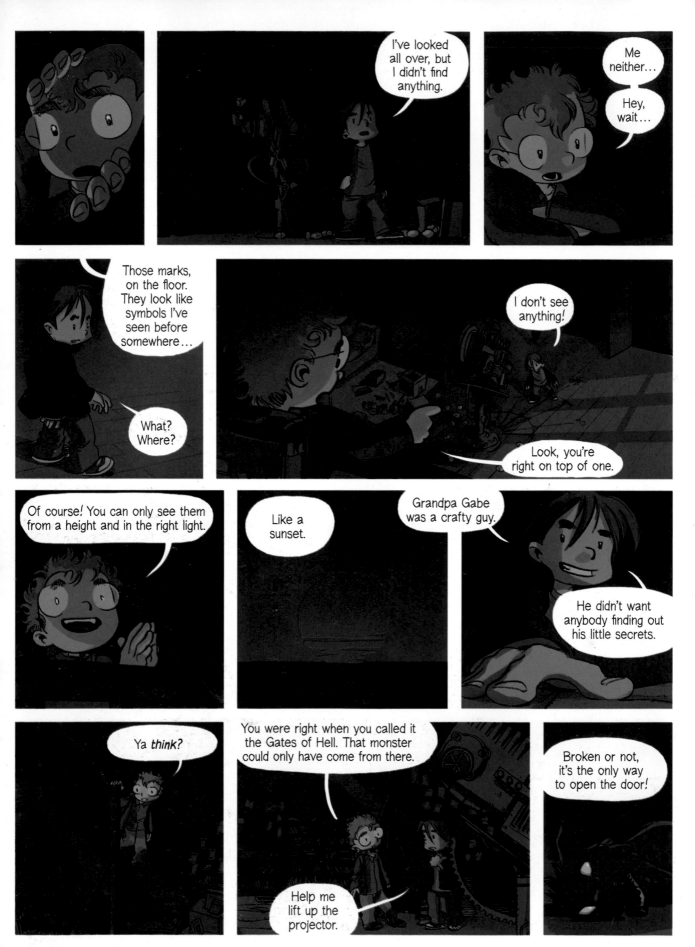

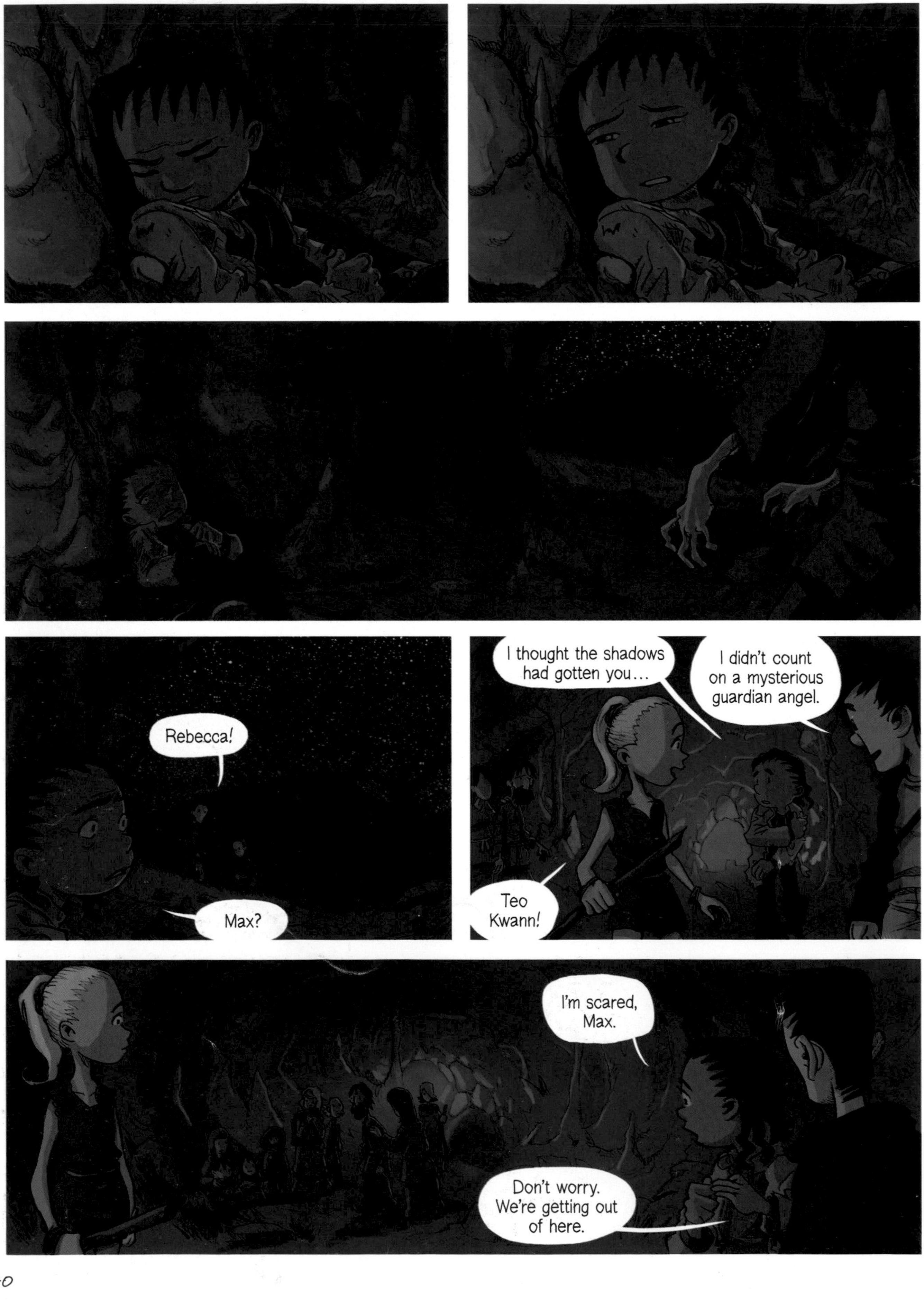
Rebecca!
Max?
I thought the shadows had gotten you...
I didn't count on a mysterious guardian angel.
Teo Kwann!
I'm scared, Max.
Don't worry. We're getting out of here.

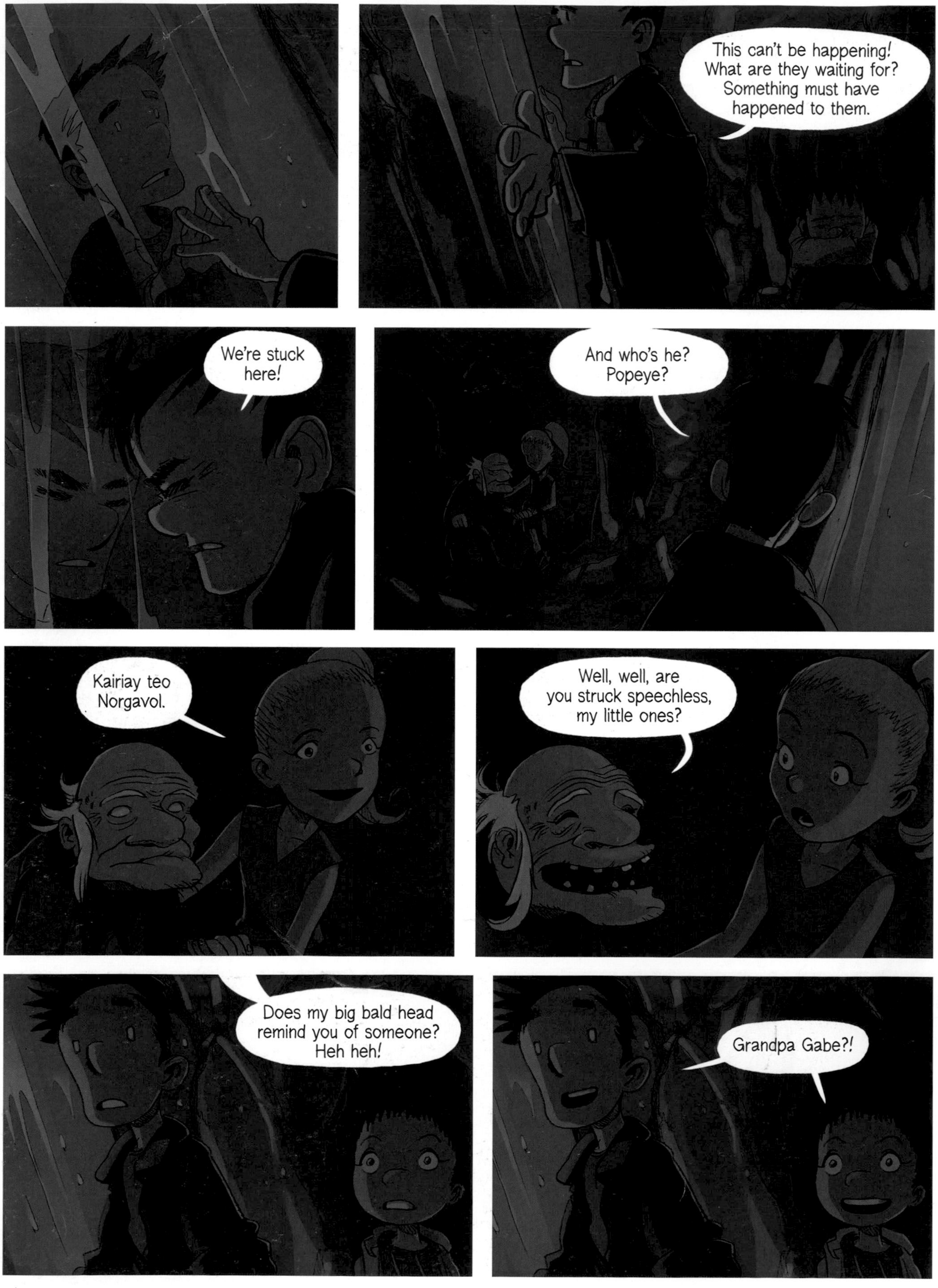
This can't be happening! What are they waiting for? Something must have happened to them.
We're stuck here!
And who's he? Popeye?
Kairiay teo Norgavol.
Well, well, are you struck speechless, my little ones?
Does my big bald head remind you of someone? Heh heh!
Grandpa Gabe?!

43

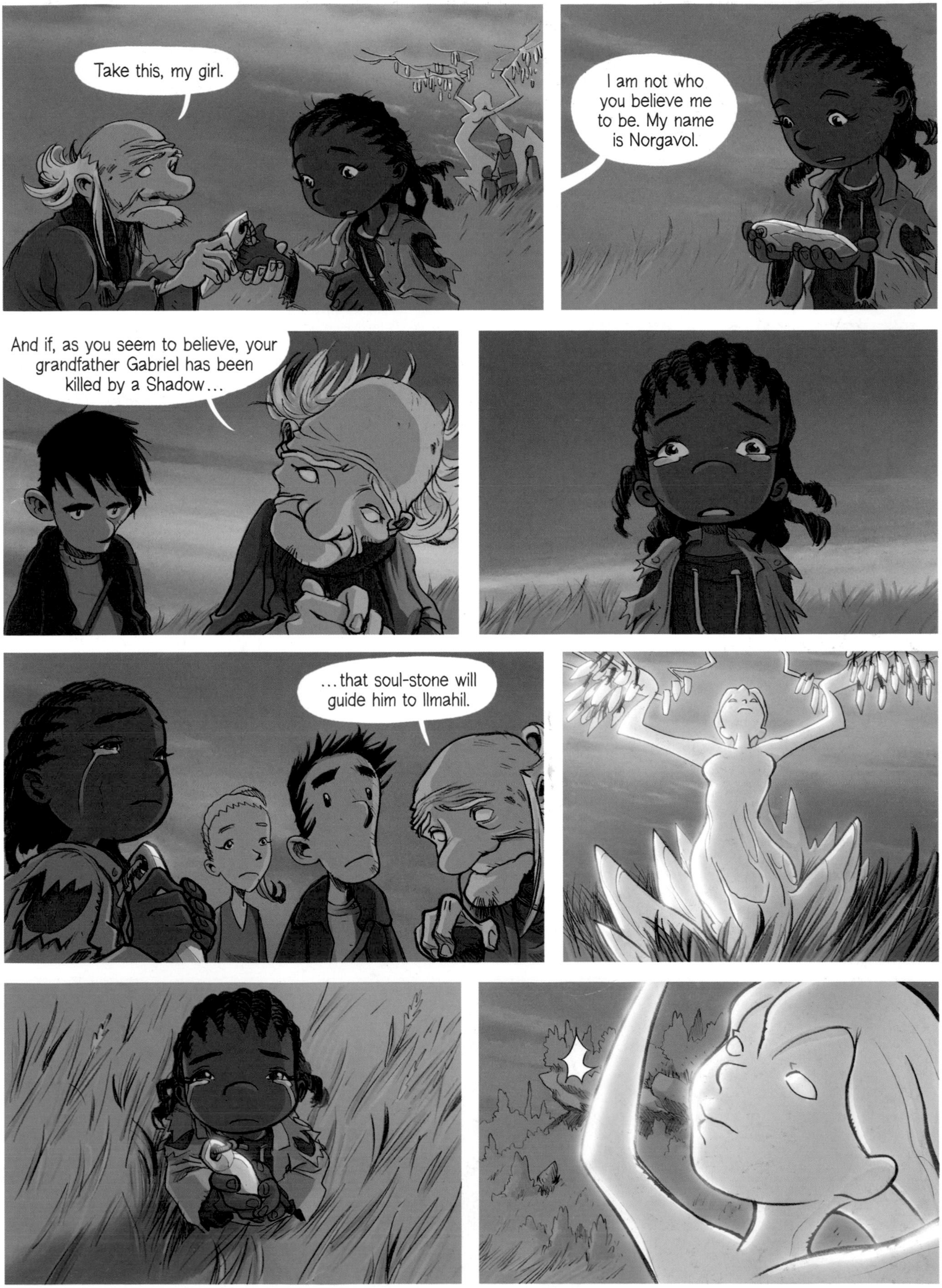
Take this, my girl.
I am not who you believe me to be. My name is Norgavol.
And if, as you seem to believe, your grandfather Gabriel has been killed by a Shadow…
…that soul-stone will guide him to Ilmahil.

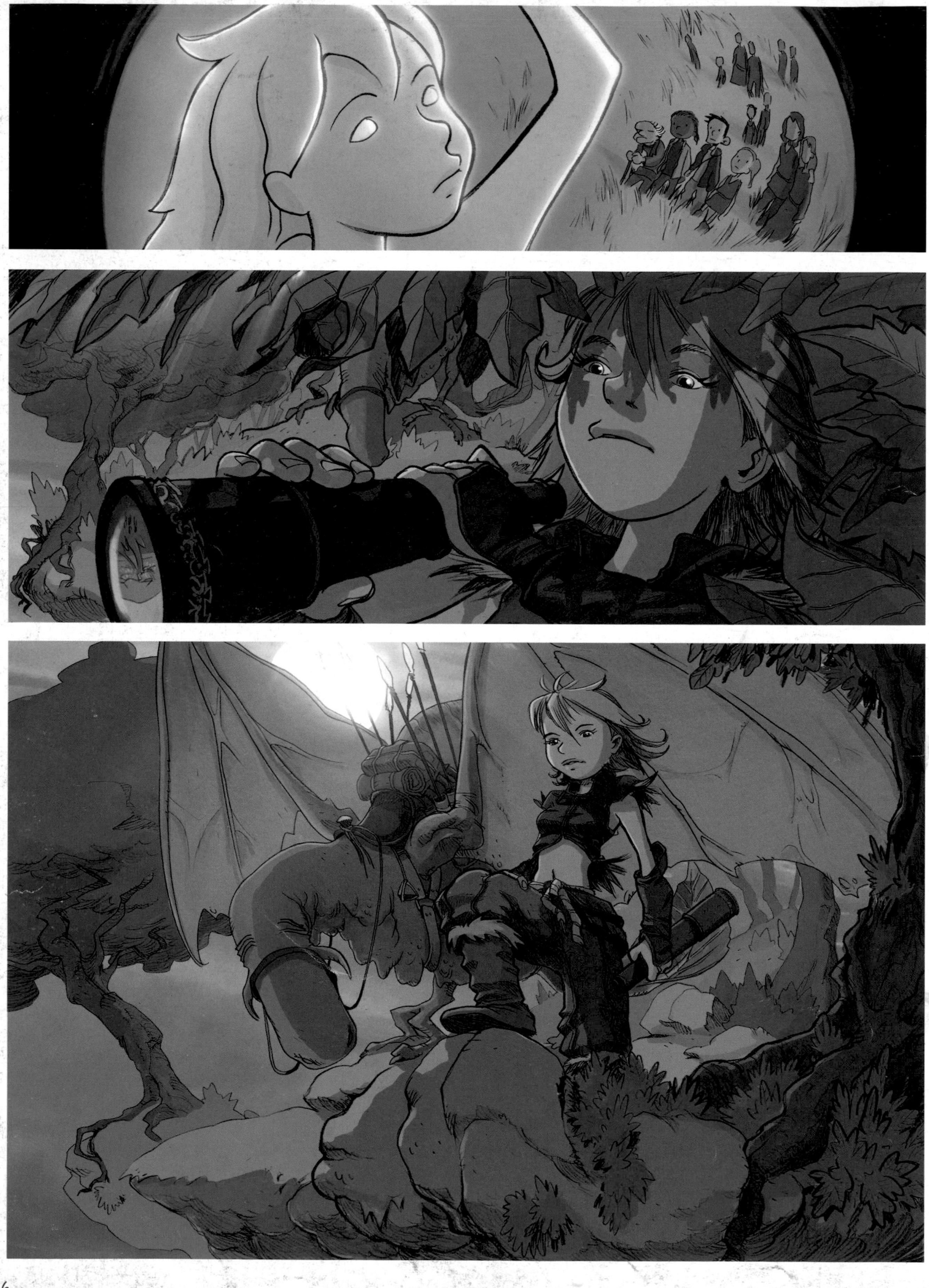

Next Episode...

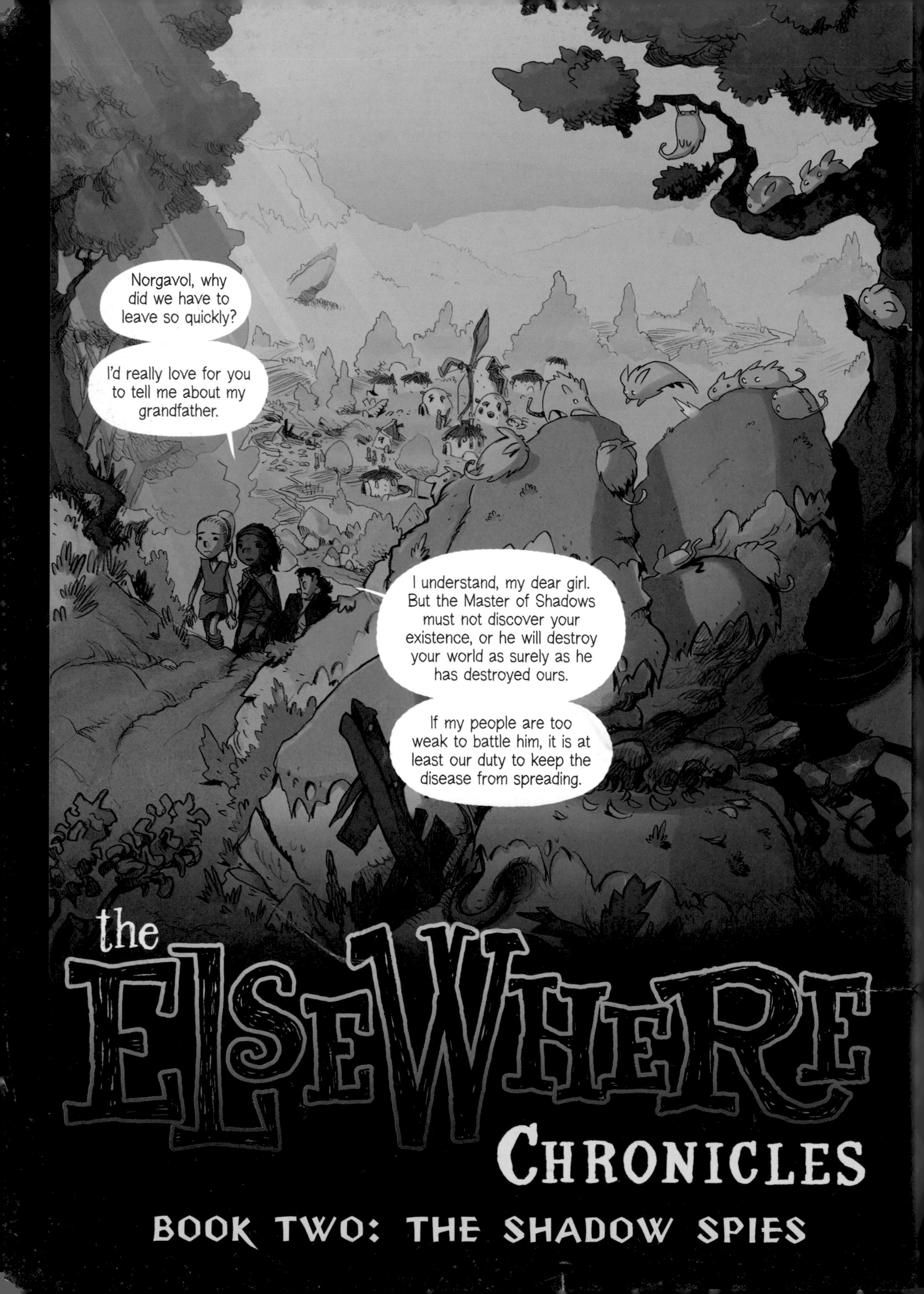
Norgavol, why did we have to leave so quickly?
I'd really love for you to tell me about my grandfather.
I understand, my dear girl. But the Master of Shadows must not discover your existence, or he will destroy your world as surely as he has destroyed ours.
If my people are too weak to battle him, it is at least our duty to keep the disease from spreading.
the ElseWhere Chronicles
BOOK TWO: THE SHADOW SPIES

Art by Bannister
Story by Nykko
Colors by Jaffré
Translation by Carol Klio Burrell

First American edition published in 2009 by Graphic Universe™.
Published by arrangement with S.A. DUPUIS, Belgium.

Graphic Universe™
A division of Lerner Publishing Group, Inc.
241 First Avenue North
Minneapolis, MN 55401 U.S.A.

Website address: www.lernerbooks.com

Library of Congress Cataloging-in-Publication Data

Bannister. [Passage. English]
The shadow door / art by Bannister ; story by Nykko ; [colors by Jaffré ;
translation by Carol Klio Burrell]. — 1st American ed.
p. cm. — (The ElseWhere chronicles ; bk. 1)
Summary: Four friends discover a movie projector that opens a passageway into
a world threatened by creatures of shadow, where their only weapon is light.
ISBN: 978-0-7613-4459-9 (lib. bdg. : alk. paper)
1. Graphic novels. [1. Graphic novels. 2. Horror stories.] I. Nykko. II. Jaffré.
III. Burrell, Carol Klio. IV. Title.
PZ7.7.B34Sh 2009
741.5'973—dc22   2008039442

Manufactured in the United States of America
1 2 3 4 5 6 - BP - 14 13 12 11 10 09

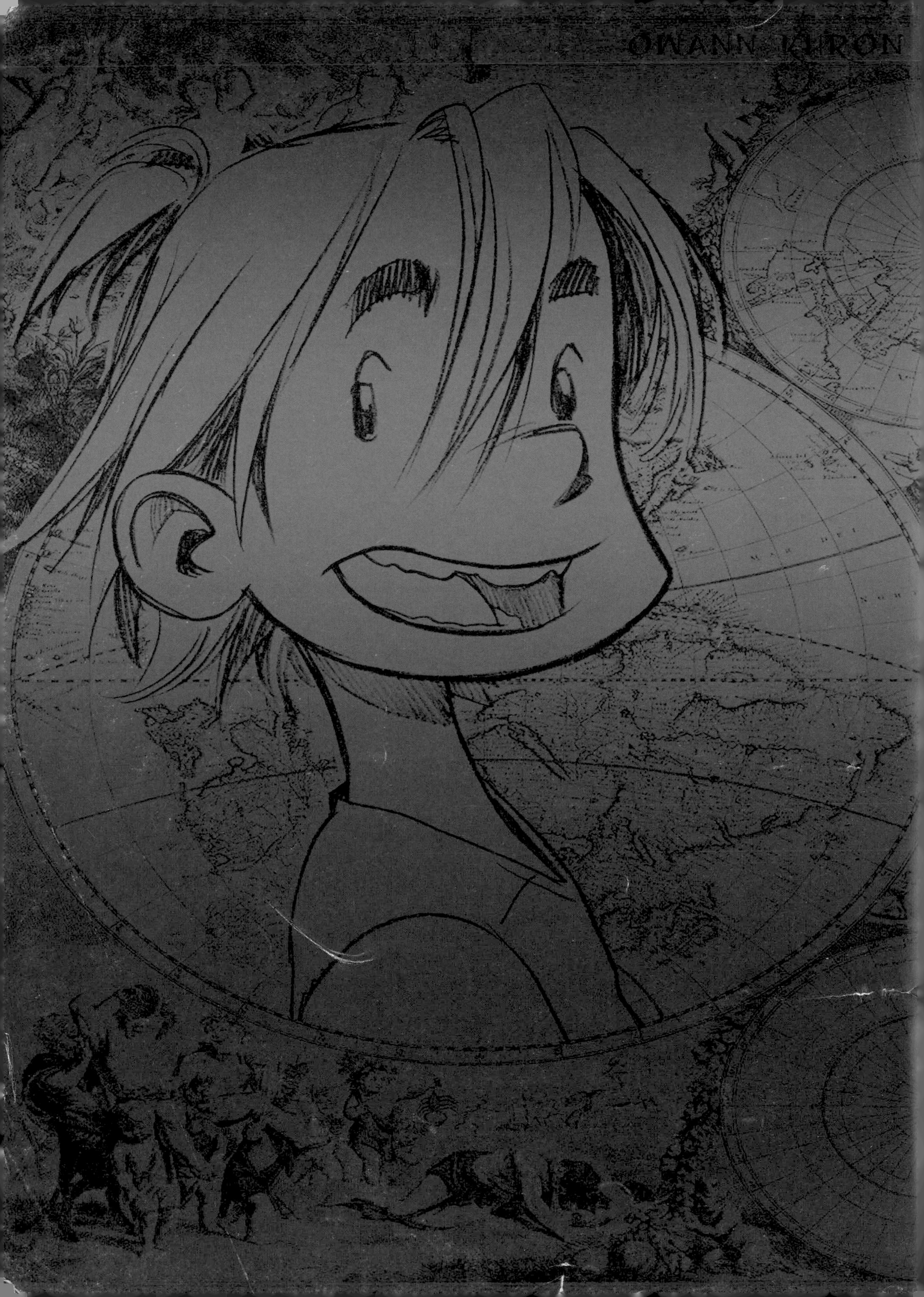

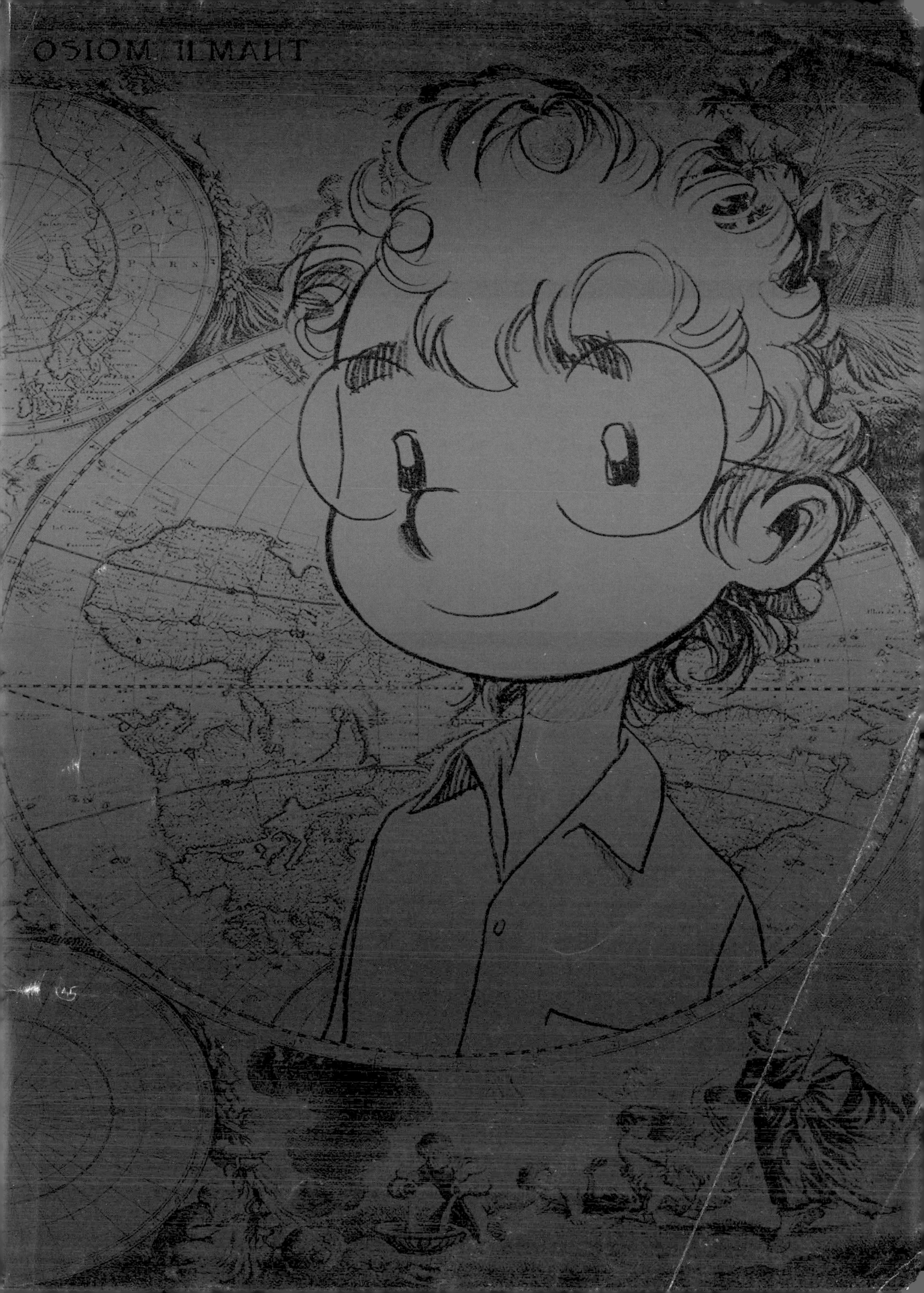